WHERE THE MISTLETOE GROWS

By Poppy Garland

Table of Contents

Dedication

For anyone who has ever wondered if you can go home again.

And for those who know the magic isn't in the leaving or the returning, but in the love that waits for you, always.

A Special Note From

Poppy Garland

Dear Reader,

There is a special kind of magic that exists only in the heart of a small town at Christmas. It's in the warm glow of the streetlights on fresh-fallen snow, the scent of cinnamon and pine, and the quiet joy of being surrounded by people who have known you your whole life.

Writing this story was like coming home for me. I hope that in the pages of Evergreen Hollow, you find a place of comfort and warmth. I hope you cheer for Holly and Noel, for their second chance, and for the beautiful, messy, wonderful journey of finding your way back to the person you were always meant to be.

Thank you for spending your time with this story. I wish you and yours the most wonderful, warm, and jolly holiday season, filled with love, laughter, and a little bit of magic.

Merry Christmas,

Poppy Garland

Prologue

Ten Years Earlier

The old covered bridge was their cathedral. On a crisp October afternoon, with the last of the autumn leaves clinging to the trees like fiery jewels, sixteen-year-old Noel Bishop pressed the tip of his pocketknife into the weathered wood of the window railing. Holly Sutton stood beside him, her head resting on his shoulder, their breaths misting in the cold air.

He carefully carved the last curve of a lopsided heart around their initials: **NB + HS**.

"There," he said, his voice full of a solemn, teenage gravity. "Now it's official. Part of the town's history."

"My dad is going to kill you for vandalizing town property," she laughed, but her fingers laced through his, holding on tight.

"It's not vandalism," he argued, turning to her, his eyes full of a fierce, brilliant sincerity that made her heart ache. "It's a promise. A blueprint." He gestured with the knife toward the town twinkling in the valley below them. "I'm going to go away, and I'm going to learn how to build things, real things. And then I'm coming back here, for you. And we're going to build a life so beautiful it'll make this whole valley jealous."

Holly looked at his face, at the raw, hopeful dream in his eyes, and she believed him with every fiber of her being. This love felt as solid and enduring as the old bridge itself. It was the foundation of everything.

"I'll be waiting," she whispered, sealing their promise with a cold-nosed, heartfelt kiss.

She believed their blueprint was foolproof, their foundation unbreakable. She had no way of knowing that sometimes, even the strongest structures can be brought down not by a dramatic, explosive force, but by the slow, silent erosion of a single, forgotten promise.

Part 1

The Frost

Chapter 1

The Ticking Clock on Main Street

The first breath of dawn over Evergreen Hollow was the color of a steel blade cold and sharp. Inside *The Rolling Pin*, however, it was warm. The air, thick with the scent of cinnamon, cardamom, and the sweet, yeasty promise of rising dough, formed a shield against the coming November chill. For Holly Sutton, this symphony of warmth and sugar was the only alarm clock she had ever needed.

Her hands, dusted with a fine white powder, worked a pliant mound of brioche dough on the floured oak table. Push, fold, turn. Push, fold, turn. It was a rhythm she knew better than her own heartbeat a legacy passed down from her grandmother, whose hands had worked this very same table for fifty years. The bakery was Holly's inheritance, her sanctuary, and lately, her gilded cage.

Tick-tock... tick-tock... tick-tock...

Grandma Sutton's old regulator clock, mounted on the far wall, measured out the morning. To anyone else, it was a comforting rhythm. To Holly, each tick was a countdown. She glanced up from her work, her gaze drifting past the steamy front window to the quiet square outside. Main Street was still asleep, its Victorian-era lamps casting a soft, lonely glow on the empty pavements.

Her eyes settled on the building directly across from her Henderson's Hardware. Or rather, the ghost of it. The windows were dark and papered over from the inside, the cheerful red paint of the sign peeling to reveal weathered gray wood beneath. It had closed in August. Before that, it was the bookshop. Before that, the little antique store. The town was becoming a collection of ghosts fond memories with nothing new to replace them.

Push, fold, turn. Her rhythm faltered. This was why she'd poured every spare minute, every ounce of her energy over the past month, into the contest. It was a flimsy, glittering lifeline but it was the only one they had.

The bell above the door chimed, a bright, cheerful sound cutting through the quiet hum of the ovens. Mayor Thompson bustled in, his round cheeks already rosy from the cold, bringing with him a gust of crisp autumn air.

"Smells like heaven in here, Holly," he said, his voice a familiar, booming comfort. "Don't suppose you've got a maple scone and a large coffee for a man trying to save a town?"

"For you, George? Always." Holly smiled, wiping her hands on her apron as she moved toward the counter. "The scones just came out. How are the nerves on the town council this morning still rattling?"

The mayor sighed as she handed him a steaming cup and a pastry in a waxed paper bag. "Like chestnuts in a tin can. Frank Henderson's convinced we're wasting time and money. Says we should be courting another big-box store for the old mill, not stringing up lights like we're in some kind of movie."

"This isn't just about lights, and he knows it," Holly said firmly. She gestured toward a chaotic but organized pile of paperwork on the counter neatly drawn sketches of wreath placements and lighting schemes pinned to a corkboard behind it. "That hundred-thousand-dollar grant from the *America's Most Festive Town* contest could keep Henderson's own sister from having to sell her diner. It could help the garage get a new roof before winter caves it in. It could mean we don't have another empty storefront by spring."

George took a large bite of his scone, nodding as he chewed. "You don't have to convince me. It's the others they want a sure thing." He sipped his coffee, his eyes kind but worried. "The submission photos are due December eighteenth. That's not a lot of time to create a miracle."

Tick-tock... tick-tock...

The clock on the wall seemed louder. Forty-one days. Forty-one days to weave together a Christmas spectacle so magical it could convince a panel of judges a hundred miles away that their tiny, struggling town was the most festive place in the country. Forty-one days to prove that the heart of Evergreen Hollow was still beating.

"It'll get done," Holly said, the words feeling heavier than the fifty-pound bag of flour she'd hauled from the pantry an hour ago. "Tradition and community spirit have to count for something."

After the mayor left with a final, encouraging nod, the bell over the door began a near-constant jingle as the morning rush descended. This was Holly's favorite part of the day the brief time when the bakery became the town's living room. She moved in a familiar dance between the pastry case, the coffee machine, and the register, a kind word and a custom order ready for everyone.

"The usual, Mr. Hemlock?" she asked, already grabbing a plain black coffee and a molasses cookie for the elderly man whose gruff exterior couldn't quite hide his sweet tooth.

"Only if it's fresh," he grumbled, though he'd asked the same question and gotten the same answer every morning for twenty years. "Still going on with this contest foolishness, are we? My taxes paying for tinsel and glitter while the potholes on Cedar Lane could swallow a small car."

"The contest doesn't cost you a dime, Silas. It's all volunteer work," Holly said patiently. "And if we win, we'll have more than enough to pave Cedar Lane twice over."

He grunted, taking his cookie. "We'll see," he muttered, but as he left, he dropped an extra five dollars into the donation jar labeled *Town Christmas Fund* on the counter. Holly smiled to herself. That was Evergreen Hollow in a nutshell complaining all the way to the finish line, but always showing up to help push.

The door chimed again, and Zara Mitchell breezed in, a whirlwind of colorful yarn and kinetic energy. Her purple-streaked hair was a vibrant slash against the muted tones of the morning.

"Don't listen to that old badger," Zara said, leaning against the counter as Holly prepared her latte. "I saw him untangling the lights on his porch yesterday. He's more excited than anyone." She lowered her voice. "So, how's the general of our tinsel army holding up? You look like you've wrestled a bag of flour and lost."

Holly laughed, a genuine, tired sound. "Something like that. I was up until two sketching out the final plans for the gazebo. My brain is ninety percent gingerbread schematics at this point."

"You need a break. A real one. Not a five-minute coffee nap," Zara said, her sharp eyes scanning Holly's face with concern. As the owner of *The Tangled Skein*, the town's beloved yarn shop, Zara was an expert at spotting the knots people tied themselves into. "We haven't had a movie night in months. Come over tonight. I've got that terrible Christmas prince movie you love and a bottle of wine that isn't half bad."

"I can't," Holly said automatically. "I have to inventory the town's entire collection of dusty, decade-old Christmas decorations in the community hall basement."

"Cancel. The dust bunnies can wait," Zara insisted. "You're running on fumes, Hol. You can't save this town if you burn yourself out."

"I'm fine," Holly said, forcing a bright smile that didn't quite reach her eyes. "Once we get the main displays up, I'll relax."

Zara took her latte, her expression unconvinced. "Famous last words. Just… text me if you need a rescue team."

After the morning rush cleared, leaving behind the lingering scent of coffee and perfume, Holly knew she couldn't put off her errand any longer. She needed to deposit the week's earnings at the bank. Pulling off her flour-dusted apron, she entrusted the counter to Betty, her cheerful part-time helper, and stepped out onto Main Street.

The November air was colder than she'd expected, and she pulled her worn wool coat tighter. The street was no longer empty, but the weekday foot traffic was sparse. It gave her an unobstructed view of the problems she was trying so hard to fix. Her gaze caught on the old bookshop the place where she and Zara had spent countless teenage afternoons, where the air had smelled of paper and possibility. Now, a stark *For Lease* sign was taped to the inside of the glass. Ten years ago, they had painted a winter scene on that very window for the holidays. She could still feel the phantom chill of the glass under her palm the warmth of a boy's hand over hers as he showed her how to shade the snow on a cartoon reindeer's antlers. He had a laugh that could make even the sourest shop owner smile.

She pushed the memory down, a familiar ache tightening in her chest. He was a ghost too and she had no time for ghosts of any kind.

As she rounded the corner, she saw exactly who she didn't want to see. Frank Henderson stood with his arms crossed, staring up at the peeling sign of his family's defunct hardware store. He was a tall, severe man whose optimism seemed to have closed down right along with his business.

"Morning, Frank," Holly said, her tone resolutely pleasant.

He turned, his gaze sharp. "Holly. Just the person. I was in the council meeting with George this morning. I want you to know I think this contest is a fool's errand."

Holly stopped, her hand tightening on the deposit bag in her pocket. "It's a chance that's more than we've had in a long time."

"It's a fantasy," he countered, stepping closer. His voice was low but heavy with bitterness. "You think a few pretty lights are going to solve real problems? We need industry. We need jobs. We don't need a parade. You're selling people false hope getting them to waste time and energy on a lottery ticket."

"Hope isn't a waste of time, Frank. It's the only thing some people have left," she shot back, her voice firm. "And it's not just lights. It's about reminding ourselves what this town is what it can be. It's about showing our kids this is a place worth fighting for, not abandoning."

The last word hung in the air between them, sharper than she intended. She saw a flicker of something hurt, maybe in his eyes before they hardened again.

"Sentiment doesn't pay the bills," he said before turning his back and walking away.

The encounter left her hands trembling slightly. She took a deep breath, the cold air burning her lungs, and continued to the bank. Frank's words stung because a small, tired part of her feared he might be right. What if it was all for nothing?

Back in the warm sanctuary of *The Rolling Pin*, the scent of cinnamon and sugar felt less like comfort and more like a challenge. She walked past the counter, past the cooling racks of scones and muffins, to the large oak table in the back that she had commandeered as her contest headquarters.

She unrolled a huge sheet of butcher paper the grand schematic for the town square. Her usually neat handwriting was now a frantic scrawl of notes and measurements. But the drawings that was where her heart lived. She'd sketched a vision of Evergreen Hollow that was pure magic: a skating rink in the center, built and maintained by volunteers; a *Parade of Trees* where every family and business could decorate their own small pine; a memory lane leading to the town hall, with illuminated photographs from the archives showing Christmases past.

Her plans weren't slick or modern they were handmade, homespun, and deeply personal. They were everything she believed in. They were the opposite of a lottery ticket; they were a testament to hard work and shared history. This was her answer to Frank Henderson. This was her reason for fighting.

Her gaze fell on her reflection in the dark glass of a display case. A smudge of flour streaked her cheek like war paint. Her blonde hair was piled into a messy bun, and there was a weariness in her blue eyes that the confrontation with Frank had etched a little deeper. This was the life she had chosen or rather, the life that had chosen her.

She looked from the detailed, hopeful drawing spread before her to the regulator clock on the wall. Its long pendulum swung back and forth a patient, relentless metronome. The ticking filled the quiet bakery.

Forty-one days. The clock was ticking. And Holly Sutton, fueled by equal parts frustration and faith, would not let time run out.

Chapter 2

Grandma Sutton's Ledger

The small office at the back of the bakery was more of a large closet, crammed with a lifetime's worth of baking history. Sacks of specialty flour rye, spelt, buckwheat now too expensive to use, were stacked against one wall like sleeping sentinels. Shelves overflowed with cookbooks, their spines cracked and pages stained with vanilla, chocolate, and the ghostly fingerprints of her grandmother. Tucked in the corner, beneath a framed photo of a smiling, flour-dusted woman with Holly's same blue eyes, stood a small, sturdy wooden desk. It was Holly's least favorite place in the world.

Here, there was no warm, forgiving scent of bread. The air smelled of old paper, ink, and the faint, metallic tang of worry. This was where the magic of the bakery met the cold, hard reality of its finances. And tonight, reality was hitting harder than usual. The cheerful energy from the morning rush had long since faded, leaving behind a silence that felt heavy and accusing.

With a sigh that seemed to come from her very bones, she pulled the heavy, leather-bound ledger from the top drawer. Its cover was worn smooth, the words *The Rolling Pin* embossed in faded gold leaf. Grandma Sutton's Ledger. It held a meticulous, handwritten record of the bakery's accounts going back thirty years. Her grandmother's script was an elegant, looping cursive each entry a mark of pride and prosperity. Holly's own entries, beginning two years ago, were small, tight, and purely functional. Lately, they'd been dominated by the angry slash of red ink.

She turned to the current month, the page a battlefield of black and red. The numbers told a story that no amount of cinnamon could sweeten. The cost of everything butter, sugar, flour, electricity had climbed relentlessly. Her weekly profits, once healthy and predictable, had shrunk to a terrifyingly thin margin. She could raise prices, of course. Any business consultant would tell her that was the first and most obvious step. But that consultant wouldn't know the faces behind the transactions.

How could she charge Mrs. Gable, a widow on a fixed income, fifty cents more for the sourdough she'd bought every other day for two decades, ever since her husband passed? Her grandmother had always made sure a loaf was ready for her a small, steady comfort in a life that had been upended. And how could she tell the high school kids who crowded in after class, their laughter a bright, welcome sound in the quiet afternoons, that their favorite chocolate chip cookies were now out of reach? She remembered being one of them, pooling change with Noel to buy a single, giant cookie to share on their walk home.

That was the heart of her dilemma. *The Rolling Pin* wasn't just a business; it was a community institution, an anchor on Main Street. Her grandmother had run it that way, often trading a loaf of bread for a promise of payment next week a system she'd called the "honor roll." She donated pastries to the church bake sale without a second thought and always kept a day-old basket for struggling families. Holly had tried to maintain that same spirit, that generosity of heart, but it was a luxury she was quickly running out of.

Her finger traced a line item from last week: *Emergency Plumber - $450.* The old pipes beneath the sink had burst with a dramatic groan, flooding the floor and nearly ruining a fifty-pound bag of sugar she'd managed to save just in time. The week before, it was the oven thermostat another three hundred dollars she hadn't budgeted for which had left her with a morning's worth of burnt, unsellable croissants. The building was old, and like the town itself, it felt as though it was slowly, expensively falling apart around her. Each repair was another unexpected wave, and she was struggling to keep her head above water.

Flipping back a few pages, she stopped at a summary from five years ago. The black ink was bold, confident. The bakery had been thriving. Tourism was stronger then. She remembered autumns when a river of tourists flowed through town for the foliage, their cars lining Main Street. They'd wander in, charmed by the old-fashioned bell and the scent of fresh bread, leaving with bags of apple cider donuts and maple scones. In winter, skiers heading to the nearby mountains would stop in for coffee and pastries to warm their hands. But now, a new bypass diverted most of that traffic a mile north of town, and the few tourists who came preferred the larger, commercial towns one exit down the highway towns with outlets and chain restaurants. Evergreen Hollow, with its quiet charm, was being overlooked.

The numbers didn't lie. At this rate, with the deep cold of winter approaching and utility bills set to climb, she had three months maybe four, if she was lucky and nothing else broke. By spring, she would face an impossible choice: take out a crippling loan that would chain her to this desk for life, sell the bakery her grandmother had poured her soul into, or close its doors for good. The thought sent a chill through her that had nothing to do with November. The contest grant wasn't just about saving the town it was about saving herself.

The sharp buzz of her phone made her jump. A text from Zara.

Zara: Have you been consumed by dust bunnies? Send proof of life. Or at least tell me you've stopped staring at that cursed ledger.

Holly: Still here. Ledger's as cursed as ever. Think I've discovered a new shade of red.

Zara: Step away from the ledger. I'm serious, Hol. Come over. I'll make popcorn.

Holly: Can't. Too much to do.

Zara: Liar. You're sitting there beating yourself up. You know what your grandmother would say? She'd tell you to close the book, have a cookie, and figure it out in the morning.

Holly looked up at the photo on the wall. Her grandmother was laughing, a smudge of flour on her cheek identical to the one Holly often wore. She had been a woman of fierce optimism and quiet strength. She'd survived two recessions and a fire that nearly destroyed the building in the seventies. Holly closed her eyes, and for a moment, the musty scent of paper gave way to the rich aroma of melting chocolate. She was twelve again, standing on a stool in this very room, watching her grandmother make a new entry in the ledger.

"See, Holly-berry," her grandmother had said, her voice warm as a fresh-baked muffin. She pointed a flour-dusted finger at a column of neat black numbers. "Every loaf of bread, every cookie, every scone they all tell a story. This one," she'd said, tapping a line, "paid for the new sign out front. And this one helped the Hemlocks pay for their son's football uniform.

This isn't just about money, sweetheart. It's a record of our community. It's a book of kindness."

Young Holly had looked from the book to her grandmother's smiling face. "But what about the red numbers?" she'd asked.

Her grandmother's smile never faltered. "Ah, the red numbers. They're just the story asking for a different ending. They're a challenge. They mean we have to be a little smarter, a little kinder, a little more creative. They're the parts where we add a little more sugar." She'd closed the book then and handed Holly a warm, gooey brownie. "There's no problem a little butter and sugar can't solve, Holly-berry."

The memory faded, leaving Holly in the silent office with the phantom taste of chocolate on her tongue. Her grandmother had made it sound so simple. But she had never faced a sea of red ink this vast. The story the ledger told now felt like it was hurtling toward a tragic ending.

Frustrated, Holly pushed the ledger away. Her gaze landed on a dusty wooden box tucked beneath the desk a time capsule she rarely dared to open. Tonight, though, the past didn't feel any more daunting than the future. Kneeling, she lifted the lid, revealing a stack of neatly organized sketchbooks. Not her grandmother's, but her own.

She pulled one out, its cover a faded navy blue. The pages were filled with architectural drawings a forgotten language her hands had once spoken fluently. There were blueprints for fantastical homes built into hillsides, designs for sleek, modern libraries with glass ceilings, and page after page of cityscapes, both real and imagined. This had been her dream before the bakery became her life the dream she'd shared with Noel Bishop. Every line, every angle, felt like a message from a different person a girl who was fearless, who believed blueprints could shape the world.

Her fingers paused on a page worn soft at the edges. It showed a grand, open-air pavilion designed for the town square, its roof shaped like overlapping holly leaves elegant and whimsical. In the corner, in Noel's sharp handwriting, were the words: *The Evergreen Project Sutton & Bishop, Lead Architects.*

They had been eighteen, sitting on the hood of his beat-up Ford, parked at the scenic overlook above town. The plans were spread between them under the car's dim dome light, the whole of Evergreen Hollow twinkling below like a fallen constellation.

"The support beams have to be steel," he'd said, his voice buzzing with excitement. He traced the lines with his finger. "But we'll wrap them in local oak so it feels strong and rooted, like it grew right out of the ground."

"And the roof panels," Holly had added, catching his enthusiasm, "should be translucent. In winter, the snow will make the light soft and glowing inside like being in a snow globe."

He'd looked at her then, eyes brighter than the town lights below. "See? That's why we're a team. I see the bones; you see the magic."

That night, they'd talked for hours, convinced they could redesign the world, starting with their small corner of it. He was the one who'd encouraged her to fill those sketchbooks, who'd bought her drafting pencils for her seventeenth birthday. He saw her talent and made her believe in it. He was going to be the architect; she, the designer. Together, they were going to build things that mattered.

A faint, bitter smile touched her lips. He had gone on to do it just differently. She'd seen his name in an architectural magazine a few years ago under "Rising Stars in Brand Experience Design." It featured a high-tech holiday installation he'd created for a luxury department store in Chicago. The photos showed something cold, brilliant, and impersonal a forest of glowing, geometric trees pulsing in perfect synchronization. Beautiful, perhaps, but lifeless. All bones, no magic. A far cry from the community-centered projects they'd once dreamed up on bakery napkins.

She closed the sketchbook, the sound echoing in the quiet room. She had chosen a different path. She hadn't built towers of glass and steel; she'd built towers of flour and sugar. She hadn't designed grand spaces; she'd preserved a small, warm one. She had stayed. He had left. Simple and complicated all at once.

But staring at the sea of red ink, she wondered if she'd made the right choice. Had she stayed to honor her grandmother's legacy or because she was afraid? Afraid to follow him, afraid to compete in his shiny world, afraid to fail and come home empty-handed. The truth, she admitted in the lonely silence, was probably a messy mix of all three. He had called once, excited about an internship, and she, with her grandmother's diagnosis weighing heavy, had only heard him slipping further away. She'd built a wall of fear and duty and never told him why she couldn't go.

The tick-tock of the clock from the front room was relentless. Forty days now.

Putting the sketchbook back, she shoved the box beneath the desk, burying the past once more. She couldn't afford to dwell on the ghost of the girl who drew buildings. That girl had no bills to pay, no town to save.

Holly turned back to the ledger, her resolve crystallizing. She would not let this place fail. She'd pour every drop of her forgotten creativity and every ounce of her stubborn Sutton spirit into winning that contest. Frank Henderson could call it a fantasy but fantasies were all she had left. She would fight for the bakery, for the town, for Mrs. Gable's sourdough and Mr. Hemlock's molasses cookie. She would fight for the simple belief that a place where people could gather for a warm scone and a kind word was worth saving.

She picked up her pen, its tip hovering over the expense column. With a steady hand, she made a new entry on a fresh line, her handwriting clear and deliberate against the surrounding chaos.

Investment: One Miracle.

The ink was black a small act of defiance on a page full of red. It wasn't a number. It wasn't a financial entry. It was a promise. She closed the ledger with a soft thud. For the first time all night, the office felt less like a cage and more like a command center.

The battle wasn't over. It had just begun.

Chapter 3

A Five-Point Plan For A Miracle

Sleep had been a fleeting, dream-tormented thing, but Holly woke before her alarm with a single, sharp-edged thought: the ink was black. That small act of defiance in her grandmother's ledger had been a turning point a match struck in the overwhelming dark of her office. Now, in the pre-dawn chill of the bakery, that tiny flame had become a frantic, consuming fire.

The dough for the morning's sourdough paid the price for her newfound resolve. She kneaded it with a fierce, punishing rhythm on the old oak table, her knuckles pressing hard into the pliant mass. Push, fold, turn. It wasn't a meditative rhythm this morning it was a battle march. Every ounce of her anxiety, every fear the ledger had unearthed, was being channeled into the work. The air, usually a comforting blanket of sweetness, now crackled with the sharp scent of dark-roast coffee and Holly's restless energy.

Between proofing cycles, she wasn't wiping counters or checking inventory. She was hunched over the small table by the window, a steaming mug at her elbow and a pen flying across a paper napkin. Ideas that had been dormant for a decade creative impulses she thought had long since faded were bubbling to the surface. The girl who drew blueprints was awake again, and though her hands were covered in flour instead of graphite, she was designing for her life. The ghosts of last night's revelations were still there, but this morning they weren't haunting her they were pushing her forward.

The bell above the door chimed, and Zara breezed in, her vibrant purple coat a welcome splash of color against the gray morning. She stopped short just inside the door, her eyes widening as she took in the scene. "Whoa," she said, pulling off her knit hat. "Okay, either you've had way too much coffee, or you're plotting to take over the world one pastry at a time. What's with the mad scientist vibe?"

"I have a plan," Holly said, her voice low and intense. She didn't look up from her furious scribbling. "It's more than just stringing up a few lights and hoping for the best. It's a real plan."

Zara walked over, peering over Holly's shoulder at the chaotic web of words and arrows on the napkin. "Looks more like the secret formula for a new kind of explosive gingerbread," she quipped gently, pulling up a stool. "Okay, General. Brief me."

Holly finally looked up, her blue eyes bright with a mixture of excitement and fear. She took a deep, steadying breath. "It's a Five-Point Plan for a Miracle," she announced, as if saying it out loud might make it more real.

She slid the napkin aside and pulled out a clean sheet of butcher paper she'd taped to the table, along with a set of colored pens she'd unearthed from a drawer. "Point One," she said, uncapping a green pen and writing the number with a flourish. "The Heartbeat of Main Street."

"Sounds poetic," Zara said, sipping the coffee Holly pushed toward her. "What does it mean?"

"It means we stop thinking about the decorations as just… decorations. They have to be personal. Every shop, every building on Main Street has to tell a story not just a generic Christmas scene, but *their* story." She started sketching as she spoke. "For your yarn shop, we don't just hang a wreath. We build a whole scene in your window out of yarn a knitted snowman, maybe a miniature Evergreen Hollow. For the diner, we recreate a scene from the fifties, when it first opened, with vintage decor. For the old, empty bookshop…" she hesitated, the memory of that window flashing in her mind. "We fill it with open books strung with fairy lights, pages glowing with quotes about hope and winter."

Zara was quiet for a moment, watching Holly's pen move. "That's… actually a really beautiful idea, Hol. But that's a ton of work. Are people going to go for it?"

"They have to," Holly insisted. "It's about showing the judges this isn't just a collection of buildings it's a collection of dreams. That's the heart of our town, and we need to show them it's still beating."

She uncapped a red pen. "Point Two: The Evergreen Gala. We're bringing it back."

Zara groaned. "The Gala? Holly, they stopped doing that fifteen years ago because it was a logistical nightmare. The last time, half the town's electrical grid blew out when they lit the tree."

"That's because they didn't have a plan," Holly countered, sketching the town square. "This time, we do. We don't just light the tree we make it an all-day event, the first Saturday of December. A real skating rink not just a flooded patch of grass in the center. The high school woodshop builds the frame, the fire department floods it, the church choir leads the carols, your mom runs the bake sale, and The Rolling Pin provides free hot chocolate for everyone. It's a full-day, immersive experience. The kind people remember the kind that ends up in the contest magazine's photo spread."

"Okay, okay, I see the vision," Zara said, holding up her hands in surrender. "But permits, insurance, volunteers… it's a mountain of work."

"I know. But a gala says we're celebrating, not just surviving. It sends a message of confidence."

She moved to the next point, her voice gaining momentum. "Point Three: The Memory Lane Project. This is our emotional hook." She described her idea for lining the path to Town Hall with archival photos. "Huge, high-quality prints mounted on weatherproof boards, each one softly lit. When the judges walk through, they're not just walking through a town they're walking through its history. They'll see founders from the 1890s raising the first Christmas tree, our parents and grandparents skating on Miller's Pond. It makes our story undeniable. It shows we're a legacy, not a relic."

"That one I love," Zara said softly. "My grandma's in half of those pictures. People will love it."

"Exactly." Holly smiled and grabbed a blue pen. "Point Four: The Community Canvas. Frank Henderson said this was all a fantasy a lottery ticket. This proves him wrong. We'll hang a massive twenty-foot canvas on the old hardware store his building and let everyone paint on it during the Gala. The prompt will say: *What does Evergreen Hollow mean to you?* Everyone can add something: a handprint, a word, a sketch. It'll be a living testament that this is our town, and we're all part of it. No one can call it false hope when the proof is right there on Main Street."

Zara stared at the growing schematic. "A five-point plan for a miracle," she murmured. "You're actually doing it. You've thought of everything."

"Not everything," Holly said quietly. She picked up a silver pen, hesitating. Her heart began to race. "There's a Point Five. The... secret weapon."

She drew a rough sketch of the Town Hall's façade. "The building's beautiful, but at night it's just a dark block. We can't cover it in lights it's a historic landmark. But we can use light on it."

She spoke faster, the words tumbling out. "A projection. A light display. Not some flashy laser show something we create. A slow animation that tells a story. It starts with a single seed, then grows into an evergreen tree as the seasons change. Subtle, artistic... magical."

Zara stared at her, stunned. "Holly, that's not a decorator's idea. That's a designer's idea. That's... old you."

The words hit Holly like a blow. *Old you.* The girl with the sketchbooks. "I don't even know if I can still do it," she whispered, her confidence faltering. "The software, the tech it's all different now. I wouldn't know where to start."

"So learn," Zara said fiercely. "Call the rental company. Watch tutorials. Figure it out. Hol, this is the most exciting idea you've had in years. This is the part that's all you. You have to do it."

The bell over the door chimed, breaking the spell. A customer needed a dozen donuts, and the conversation paused.

But as Holly boxed the pastries, her mind was reeling. The plan felt both brilliant and impossibly huge.

After Zara left, promising to recruit volunteers, Holly stood alone over the butcher paper. The five points stared back at her a roadmap to either salvation or spectacular failure. Doubt rushed in, cold and sharp. Who was she to think she could pull this off? She was a baker, not an event planner. Not an artist. Not anymore. Frank Henderson's cynical voice echoed in her head: *A fool's errand.*

She walked to the front window, gazing at the quiet, struggling town she called home. It wasn't enough to have a plan she had to make the whole town believe in it.

Her reflection caught her eye. She saw exhaustion there, but beneath it, a spark the same spark that once dreamed of building snow globes the whole world could live inside. She heard Noel's voice, clear as if he were beside her: *"I see the bones; you see the magic."*

Maybe he was right. Maybe she *did* see the magic. And maybe it was time she showed everyone else.

Turning from the window, she strode to the community corkboard by the door, crowded with ads for babysitters and lost cats. She took a blank sheet of paper and a thick marker. In big, bold letters, she wrote:

A MIRACLE IS IN THE MAKING.

TOWN HALL MEETING – FRIDAY, 7 PM

COME BE A PART OF THE PLAN TO SAVE EVERGREEN HOLLOW.

She pinned it squarely in the center of the board. It was a declaration of war against the ghosts of the past and the doubts of the present. The plan was no longer a secret. Now, all she had to do was convince everyone else to believe in it as much as she dared to.

Chapter 4

The Consultant From Chicago

Three hundred miles away, in a city that scraped the sky, the only ticking clock Noel Bishop heard was the silent, insistent pulse of a deadline on his digital calendar. His apartment, forty-two floors above the Chicago River, was a study in controlled minimalism concrete floors, charcoal-gray furniture, and a single dramatic piece of abstract art on the wall. It was less a home and more a gallery curated for a man who was never really there. A wall of glass offered a panoramic view of the city's electric grid: a glittering, impersonal beauty Noel had once found inspiring and now barely noticed.

He stood before a holographic projector, a faint blue light illuminating his tired features. Swiping a hand through the air, he manipulated a three-dimensional rendering of a Christmas display for a flagship luxury boutique on Michigan Avenue. It was a forest of sleek, chrome-plated reindeer, their antlers branching into intricate, algorithm-generated fractals. A synchronized LED system would make them appear to gallop through a field of pure white light. It was technically brilliant, innovative, and projected to increase foot traffic by eighteen percent. It was also completely, utterly soulless.

The project was a masterpiece of *brand synergy* and *consumer engagement* words that lately tasted like ash in his mouth. He was at the top of his game, the rising star the industry magazines praised, but the game itself was beginning to feel like a gilded cage. The thrill of the pitch, the challenge of the engineering, the satisfaction of the execution all of it had faded into a monotonous, high-stakes routine. He was building beautiful, empty things for people who had everything, and the work left him hollowed out.

His phone buzzed on the granite countertop. He glanced at the caller ID: *Dad.* A familiar mix of love and guilt twisted in his gut. He hadn't been home for Christmas in five years.

"Hey, Dad," he said, forcing a cheerful tone as he collapsed onto the low-slung leather sofa.

"Noel! Just wanted to catch you. Your mother's making that lasagna you like and was wondering if you'd finally figured out how to teleport."

Noel managed a small laugh. "Working on it. Still stuck with commercial airlines for now. How are things?"

"Oh, you know. The town's still the town." His father's voice was warm, but beneath it lingered the weariness Noel knew too well. "A little quieter this year. Henderson's Hardware finally closed up for good. A real shame." There was a pause. "You know, everyone's pinning their hopes on this *Most Festive Town* contest. You should see it, Noel. Holly Sutton's got the whole town stringing up lights and painting signs. She's working her heart out, that one."

The name landed in the sterile silence of his apartment like a stone dropped into a still pond, ripples spreading instantly through him. *Holly Sutton.* He hadn't heard her name spoken aloud in years, though it had been a quiet hum in the back of his mind for as long as he could remember. He pictured her immediately blonde hair tied back, a smudge of paint on her cheek, eyes that could see magic in anything.

"That's… nice," Noel said, his voice tightening. He cleared his throat. "Good for her."

"She's a good kid. Always was," his dad continued, oblivious to the tension. "Well, listen, son. No pressure, but your mother would be over the moon if you made it home this year. Just think about it."

After he hung up, Noel stared out at the indifferent city lights. Loneliness pressed against him, deep and unrelenting. He was surrounded by millions of people, yet felt completely disconnected. His father's words echoed in his mind *She's working her heart out.* He felt a pang of something he refused to name.

As if on cue, his phone buzzed again. This time, it was an unknown number with a Vermont area code. He almost ignored it, but on a strange impulse, he answered.

"Is this Noel Bishop?" The voice was friendly, a little breathless.

"It is."

"Mr. Bishop, my name is George Thompson. I'm the mayor of Evergreen Hollow."

Noel sat up straighter, a frown creasing his brow. "Mr. Mayor. To what do I owe the pleasure?"

"Well, son, I'll get right to it. Our town is a finalist in the *America's Most Festive Town* contest. The prize money would… well, it would be a game-changer for us. Our volunteer committee is working hard, but some of the council feel we need a professional edge a sure thing. Your father mentioned you were in the business of, well, spectacular displays. The council's authorized me to offer you a consulting fee to come home and oversee the project to get us over the finish line."

Noel was stunned into silence. Go back to Evergreen Hollow to consult on a small-town Christmas display? His mind instantly catalogued the reasons it was ridiculous a backward step. It was small-time, sentimental, the polar opposite of the sleek, high-budget projects that had built his career.

But then he thought of the chrome reindeer. He thought of the hollow feeling in his chest. He thought of his mother's lasagna, the guilt baked into every layer. And he thought of Holly Sutton, working her heart out.

Maybe this was the answer. An easy win. A professional palate cleanser after the corporate grind. A way to finally go home for the holidays with a purpose to be the successful son returning to save the day. A neat, tidy narrative he could sell himself.

"Mr. Mayor," Noel said, a decision settling into place. "I'd be happy to help. Send me the details. I'll be there by the end of the week."

The drive from Burlington International Airport to Evergreen Hollow was a journey backward in time. The sleek modern lines of the city gave way to rolling hills, then to dense forests of pine and bare-limbed birch. The farther he drove, the more the polished armor of his Chicago life seemed to flake away. He saw a frozen pond and remembered falling through the ice Holly's terrified face the first thing he saw when he surfaced. He passed a dilapidated barn with a faded advertisement on its side and remembered the two of them hiding in a hayloft during a thunderstorm, whispering their dreams. He gripped the steering wheel tighter, forcing the memories back into their box. *This was a job. Nothing more.*

When he pulled onto Main Street, nostalgia hit him harder than he expected. Everything was smaller than he remembered, yet achingly familiar: the green awning of the diner, the steeple of the church, the slightly crooked town clock. But his architect's eye also caught the decay the dark, empty windows of Henderson's Hardware, the *For Lease* sign on the old bookshop. A quiet sadness clung to the edges of the town's charm. His professional instincts kicked in immediately, diagnosing problems and formulating solutions. A unified color scheme. Modern signage. A more strategic lighting plan. He could fix this. He could make it better.

He was scheduled to meet Mayor Thompson and the head of the volunteer committee at Town Hall. The community meeting room smelled of stale coffee and old wood. The mayor stood near a table with Frank Henderson. Frank looked older, his face set in permanent lines of disapproval, but he gave a curt nod when he saw Noel. This had been his idea his "sure thing."

"Noel! Glad you could make it," Mayor Thompson boomed, shaking his hand. "This is a real coup for us. Frank, you remember Noel Bishop."

"Bishop," Henderson said, his grip firm and dry. "Good to have a professional on board. We need someone who understands ROI, not just… glitter."

"The head of our committee's just grabbing some coffee and pastries for us," the mayor said, blissfully unaware of the storm about to break. "She'll be right in. A real firecracker, this one the heart and soul of the whole operation."

Noel smiled, wearing the practiced expression he used with clients. He imagined a sweet, bustling woman in her sixties perhaps the librarian or head of the historical society. He was already preparing his pitch: the gentle but firm way he'd explain that their charming, homespun ideas needed to be streamlined into a cohesive, impactful brand experience.

And then the door opened.

The woman who entered was not in her sixties. She carried a cardboard tray of steaming coffee cups and a plate of golden, sugar-dusted scones. Her blonde hair was tied in a messy bun, a stray strand falling across her forehead. Her cheeks were flushed from the cold, and her hands the ones he'd held a thousand times were dusted with flour. She looked up, scanning the room, and then her eyes found his.

For a heartbeat, the world stopped. The chatter, the smell of coffee, the ticking clock everything vanished. Noel felt the air leave his lungs in a silent rush. *Holly.* Of course it was Holly. The name his father had spoken, the name that had echoed in his mind, now stood ten feet away from him a living paradox of the girl he remembered and the woman she'd become. The carefully built walls around his heart didn't just crack; they vaporized. The confident Chicago architect disappeared, replaced by a stunned, speechless eighteen-year-old boy.

Holly's tray tilted precariously. The friendly smile she'd entered with froze, then faded into shock. Noel watched the color drain from her face. Her eyes once full of warmth and laughter were wide with disbelief and something else... something that looked like betrayal.

Mayor Thompson, oblivious, beamed. "Ah, here she is! Noel Bishop, I'd like you to meet the heart and soul of our committee the one making all this happen. This is Holly Sutton."

The name, spoken aloud between them, felt like an accusation. Holly set the tray on the table with a clatter, her movements stiff. She wiped her hand on her jeans an unconsciously familiar gesture that made Noel's chest ache and extended it.

He took it. Her skin was warm, the touch electric a jolt of ten years' worth of unspoken words and unresolved feelings.

"Bishop," she said coolly, her voice brittle and unfamiliar. Her eyes were ice. "I didn't realize you were the council's new consultant."

"Sutton," he managed, his own voice foreign. "It was a last-minute arrangement."

The air between them was thick with history and hurt. Frank Henderson watched with interest; the mayor only smiled, proud of his "dream team."

"Well, now that everyone's here, let's get started!" George said, gesturing for them to sit. "Holly, why don't you start by walking Noel through your five-point plan?"

Holly's back straightened. She glanced from the mayor to Frank's smug face, then to Noel the ghost who'd stepped out of her past and into her present. She took a steadying breath, her professional mask sliding into place, though he could see the tremor in her hands as she picked up her notes. This wasn't just a meeting anymore. It was a confrontation.

She began to speak, her tone tight but composed, outlining her vision for a heartfelt, community-driven celebration. Noel, still reeling, fell back on his only defense his professional persona. It was the one shield he had left.

When she finished describing her "Heartbeat of Main Street" concept, he replied, his voice colder than he meant it to be.

"It's a charming concept," he began, the words tasting like poison. "But from a design perspective, it's fragmented. There's no cohesive brand identity. To make an impact on the judges, we need a singular, powerful aesthetic. A more streamlined approach would be logistically efficient and visually stronger."

He saw the flicker of pain in her eyes before it hardened into fury. He hadn't meant to wound her it was just what he did. It was his job.

But in that gut-wrenching moment, he realized he had done something far worse. He had just dismissed her heart as *inefficient.* And the look on her face told him everything: the boy who had once promised to build her dreams had come back to declare them structurally unsound.

The battle for the soul of Evergreen Hollow had just become painfully personal.

Chapter 5

Ghosts In The Gingerbread

The silence that settled over the community meeting room was cold and heavy, thick with a decade of unspoken history. Holly stood rigid, her knuckles white as she gripped her stack of notes. Noel's words echoed in the stale air streamlined, logistically efficient, brand identity. He had taken her heart, put it on a slide, and examined it under a microscope, finding it charmingly inadequate. He had looked at her magic and called it a rounding error.

From the corner of her eye, she saw Zara's hands clench into fists on the table. Mayor Thompson, bless his conflict-averse soul, attempted a wobbly smile, looking between Holly and Noel as if they were two children he might coax into sharing a toy. Frank Henderson, however, leaned back in his chair with a look of profound vindication. This was the clinical, decisive professional he had paid for the antidote to all of Holly's sentimental foolishness.

"Well!" the mayor boomed, his voice too loud for the small room. "A fresh perspective! That's what this is. Good. Holly, you were about to tell us about Point Two."

Holly took a breath, the air searing her lungs. She would not let him see how deeply his words had cut her. She would be a professional, just like he was. She forced herself to meet his gaze across the table. His eyes the same gray-blue eyes that had once looked at her drawings with wonder were guarded, his expression carefully neutral. He was a stranger in a familiar suit.

"Point Two," she said, her voice steady despite the tremor inside, "is the Evergreen Gala. A revival of an old town tradition. An all-day event on the first Saturday of December to kick off the festive season and bring the whole community together."

She laid out the vision she had so passionately described to Zara: the skating rink built by the high schoolers, the carolers, the bake sale, the free hot chocolate. She spoke of the feeling it would create the sense of shared purpose and celebration the judges would find irresistible the very thing that made Evergreen Hollow special.

When she finished, Noel didn't hesitate. He leaned forward, tapping a sleek silver pen on his leather-bound notebook. "Okay, let's break this down from a resource-allocation standpoint," he began, and Holly felt a fresh wave of cold fury. "You're proposing a significant volunteer-hour expenditure for a one-day event with a limited experiential footprint. The ROI is... questionable."

"The ROI?" Zara interrupted, unable to stop herself. "It's a Christmas festival, not a corporate merger."

Noel's gaze flickered to Zara, his expression unreadable. "It's a competition with a six-figure prize. We have to think of it like a campaign. The Gala is high-cost, high-risk. What if it rains? What if the turnout is low? I'd propose a more scalable, media-friendly alternative. A professionally curated 'Tree Lighting Moment.' We focus all our resources on one perfect hour. We bring in professional lighting, maybe a small string quartet. We create a visually stunning, highly shareable event that will play well on social media and in the judges' photo submission."

"You want to hire musicians when our fire department has a volunteer band that's been playing at town events for fifty years?" Holly asked, her voice dangerously quiet. "You want to replace a full day of our community celebrating together with one 'shareable moment'?"

"I want to win," Noel said simply, his gaze locked on hers. "You can't win a national contest with just feelings and hot chocolate."

The words were a direct hit, a callback to an argument that hadn't even happened yet. It was a rejection of everything she stood for everything the bakery represented.

"Moving on," Holly said through clenched teeth. "Point Three. The Memory Lane Project. Lining the path to Town Hall with illuminated archival photos of our town's history."

"Charming," Noel said and the word was starting to sound like the most condescending insult Holly had ever heard. "But it's passive. It relies on the judges taking the time to engage with static displays. We need to be more forward-thinking. Why not an interactive digital archive? A QR code on a single plaque that links to a professionally designed website showcasing the town's history? It's cleaner, more modern. We need to show the judges we're a town with a future, not one stuck in the past."

Stuck in the past. The irony was so thick Holly could almost choke on it. He, who had run from their past as fast as he could, was now accusing her of being trapped in it.

"Our history is our foundation," she said, her voice shaking slightly. "It's not something to be scanned with a phone. It's something to be respected."

Frank Henderson cleared his throat. "I have to agree with Mr. Bishop. This sounds much more professional. Forward-thinking."

Holly ignored him, her focus entirely on Noel. She slammed her hand down on the butcher paper. "Point Four. The Community Canvas. A direct answer to your concerns about 'feelings.' We give the community a chance to physically invest in this project to paint their hopes for this town onto a canvas for everyone to see."

"An uncontrolled variable," Noel countered instantly. "Artistically, it's a mess. You can't guarantee the quality of the final product. The brand identity we're trying to build needs to be consistent. A much better use of that prime visual real estate would be a professionally commissioned mural. We could hire an artist to paint something that incorporates the town's key visual assets the clock tower, the covered bridge into a clean, modern design. Something that says 'progress.'"

"It's not a brand!" Holly snapped, her control shattering. "It's our home! Don't you remember what a home is, Noel?"

The use of his first name the first time either of them had used it hung in the air like a gunshot. His professional mask slipped for a fraction of a second, his eyes flashing with something that looked like hurt.

"And finally," Holly said, her voice dripping with sarcastic fury, "my 'secret weapon.' Point Five. An animated light projection on the face of the Town Hall. A story, told in light."

She explained the idea, her voice trembling with the effort of not screaming. She described the seed, the growing tree, the changing seasons. As she spoke, she saw a flicker of the old Noel in his eyes the designer, the creator. He leaned forward, genuinely intrigued.

"The concept has potential," he admitted, and for a wild second, Holly felt a sliver of hope. But then the corporate architect returned. "The render times would be significant. We'd need to outsource the animation to a firm with the right processing power. We'd have to do a cost-per-lumen analysis on the projectors to ensure optimal brightness without violating historical society regulations. I know a vendor in Boston who could probably give us a good deal on a stock animation package. Something with snowflakes or tasteful geometric patterns."

That was it. The final, unforgivable blow. A stock animation package. He had taken her most personal, most artistic, most deeply felt idea and offered to replace it with the cheapest, most soulless alternative he could find.

"I'm done," Zara said, pushing her chair back with a loud scrape. "I cannot listen to this. He's trying to turn Evergreen Hollow into a strip mall. Holly is talking about creating something with meaning, and you're talking about a balance sheet and stock animations!"

"This is exactly what we need!" Frank Henderson shot back, standing to meet Zara's glare. "A clear-eyed professional who isn't afraid to make the tough decisions not a bake sale organizer who thinks everything can be solved with a group hug."

The room erupted. Zara and Henderson argued, their voices rising. Mayor Thompson flapped his hands, pleading for calm. Through it all, Holly and Noel just stared at each other across the table, the chaos around them a faint echo of the storm raging between them.

This was her plan her miracle and he had torn it to shreds in less than twenty minutes, with a cold, detached precision that hurt more than any screaming fight could have.

"Enough," Holly said. Her voice wasn't loud, but it cut through the noise with absolute finality. Everyone stopped and looked at her.

She calmly gathered her notes, her movements deliberate. She refused to look at Noel. "This meeting is over," she said, her voice devoid of emotion. "Clearly, the committee has a new director. I'll await his streamlined, forward-thinking, professional instructions."

Without another word, she turned and walked out of the room, leaving a stunned, perfect silence in her wake.

She didn't stop walking until she was back behind the counter of The Rolling Pin, the bell over the door chiming her frantic entry. The bakery her sanctuary felt different now. Tainted. Every familiar object was a memory, every scent a ghost. The smell of cinnamon reminded her of their first kiss. The big oak table was where they had once spread out their own blueprints. The whole place was haunted by him, and now the ghost had come home and was trying to evict her. She was shaking, a deep, furious tremor that started in her chest and spread to her fingertips.

The bell chimed again. She didn't have to look up to know it was him.

"Holly," he said quietly, hesitating at the door. He looked utterly out of place in his expensive wool coat amid the cozy, flour-dusted warmth of her life.

"What do you want, Noel?" she asked, her back still to him as she rearranged a display of gingerbread cookies with jerky, obsessive movements.

"That was not how I intended for that to go."

She spun around, her eyes blazing. "What, exactly, did you intend? To march in here and systematically dismantle every idea I've had, every piece of my heart I've poured into this? Did you intend to call my life's work 'inefficient' and 'sentimental'?"

"That's not what I was doing," he said, taking a step closer. "I was doing my job. I was giving a professional analysis. These are proven strategies, Holly. This is how you win these things. I'm trying to help."

"Help?" She let out a short, incredulous laugh. "By turning our home into another one of your sterile, corporate clients? I saw the pictures of your work online, Noel. Those soulless chrome reindeer. Is that your vision for us? To strip-mine the soul of this town for a cash prize?"

His face tightened, her words hitting a nerve he hadn't expected her to find. "That's not fair. You can't win a national competition with handmade signs and a bake sale. The world is bigger than Evergreen Hollow. You have to compete on a different level."

"Oh, I forgot," she said, her voice laced with a decade of resentment. "You're the expert on the big, wide world the one who couldn't wait to leave it all behind. You abandoned our dreams then, Noel, and now you've come back to bulldoze the new ones. You don't get to do that."

"I didn't abandon them!" he shot back, his anger finally breaking through. "I went out to get the skills to make them happen! While you stayed here, hiding in this… this museum, afraid to take a single risk!"

The cruelty of his words stole her breath. She flinched, and his anger evaporated instantly, replaced by regret. But the damage was done. The chasm between them was no longer just a decade of silence it was a fresh, gaping wound.

"Get out of my bakery," she whispered, her voice trembling.

He stood there for a moment, his face a mess of conflicting emotions. Then, without another word, he turned and left, the bell over the door chiming a soft, sorrowful goodbye.

Holly was left alone in the ringing silence, her breath coming in ragged gasps. She looked around at the warm, cozy space the legacy her grandmother had left her, the life she had built. It was all so fragile. He could break it all so easily.

Her eyes landed on the tray of gingerbread men she had been arranging. They were smiling, their little icing faces cheerful and oblivious. On a raw, primal impulse, she snatched one up. With a furious, satisfying crunch, she bit its head off. The sharp, spicy sweetness was a small, childish explosion on her tongue a pathetic but deeply necessary act of defiance.

The battle was just beginning. And she would be damned if she let him win.

Chapter 6

Two Versions of A Dream

Noel Bishop didn't walk away from The Rolling Pin; he retreated. The chime of the bell behind him wasn't a gentle farewell but the sound of a door slamming shut on a conversation ten years overdue. He strode down Main Street, the cold November air doing nothing to cool the hot, unfamiliar shame churning in his gut. He was a man who prided himself on control on his ability to read a room, manage expectations, and steer any project toward success. Yet in the span of thirty minutes, he'd managed to alienate the one person whose opinion, he was horrified to admit, still mattered to him more than any client's.

He ended up at the scenic overlook the same spot where he and Holly had once parked his beat-up Ford and designed their future. He leaned against the cold stone wall, the whole of Evergreen Hollow spread out below him like a toy town nestled in the dark folds of the mountains. From up here, it was easy to see the problems with a detached architect's eye: the haphazard layout of the Christmas lights, the inconsistent signage, the lack of a central visual anchor. From up here, his logic was sound. His plan was efficient. It was the correct way to win.

So why did he feel like he'd just kicked a puppy?

"Hiding in this… this museum, afraid to take a single risk!"

His own words echoed in the quiet air ugly and cruel. He had lashed out, hitting her where he knew it would hurt most because she'd hit him first. *Soulless chrome reindeer.* She had dismissed his entire career everything he'd worked for as cold and empty. The accusation stung because, deep down, in the quiet 4 a.m. moments in his sterile Chicago apartment, he feared she was right.

He had left Evergreen Hollow with a fire in his belly, driven by a fierce ambition to prove himself worthy of their shared dreams. He'd wanted to learn how to build things that would last to return with the skills and capital to make their fantastical "Evergreen Project" a reality. But the world he'd entered was seductive. The praise, the promotions, the ever-larger budgets they had become a new kind of dream. The goal had shifted from building something meaningful to simply winning. He'd gotten so good at the game that he'd forgotten why he started playing in the first place.

He looked down at the town again. Holly wasn't hiding; she was defending. She was the keeper of the flame the one who had stayed to protect the soul of the place he had so eagerly abandoned. He'd walked back in not as her partner but as a corporate raider, talking about ROI and brand identity as if her life's work were just another asset to be leveraged. He had seen the heart in her five-point plan the messy, inefficient, beautiful heart of it all and his first instinct had been to perform a triple bypass.

A muscle in his jaw tightened. Regret was a useless emotion. He was here to do a job a job the town council had hired him for. Frank Henderson was counting on him to be the clear-eyed professional. If Holly couldn't see the logic if she was too sentimental to make the hard choices then he'd have to make them for her. For the good of the town. He told himself this, repeating it like a mantra, but it did little to soothe the ragged feeling in his chest.

This wasn't two professionals disagreeing on strategy. This was two people, once deeply connected, presenting two fundamentally different versions of a dream they'd once built together. His was a dream of progress, success, and proving his worth to the world. Hers was a dream of preservation, community, and protecting a legacy. And right now, those two dreams were at war.

He spent the next two days in a blur of relentless, professional efficiency. He rented a small temporary office in a vacant storefront and turned it into a command center. A large, high-resolution map of the town was printed and mounted, and he began pinning power sources, sightlines, and areas for "high-impact visual installations."

His first official act was to issue a new, town-wide decorating directive. He emailed it to the volunteer committee an address Holly had pointedly not provided, which he'd had to get from the mayor's office. The document was a masterpiece of corporate clarity. It outlined a unified color palette (Evergreen, Winter White, and Cranberry Red), specified the exact type and wattage of LED bulbs to be used ("for consistency and energy efficiency"), and listed approved vendors for wreaths and garlands ("to ensure brand cohesion"). It gently but firmly shelved Holly's "Heartbeat of Main Street" concept in favor of a clean, uniform look.

The reaction was immediate and icy. No one replied to the email, but the silence was deafening. Word was spreading through town like a cold wind: the slick city boy had returned, thinking their family traditions could be replaced by a style guide.

Undaunted, he moved on to the Gala. He canceled the order for the wood to build the skating rink frame, citing "potential liability issues and budget overruns." Instead, he booked the string quartet from Burlington he'd mentioned in the meeting, scheduling them for a tight forty-five-minute set on the evening of the tree lighting a performance he was already mentally branding as *An Evening of Classical Christmas.*

He felt like a general moving chess pieces making logical, winning moves. But every decision felt like a betrayal. Every email he sent was a fresh wound in a conversation he should've been having with Holly face-to-face.

On the third day, the first shipment of his "approved" decorations arrived. A massive truck pulled up on Main Street, and a team of workers began unloading dozens of boxes filled with identical, perfectly formed wreaths and spools of matching velvet ribbon. Noel stood on the pavement, arms crossed, directing the workers where to stack the boxes.

He saw curtains twitch in the shop windows. Silas Hemlock stopped on the corner, his face a mask of pure, unfiltered disgust. And then he saw Holly.

She came out of The Rolling Pin, wiping her hands on her apron, and just stood there, watching the sterile, mass-produced Christmas spirit being unloaded onto her street. She didn't look angry. She looked… heartbroken. It was a look that twisted something deep inside him.

"This is your streamlined approach?" she asked quietly as she walked toward him. She picked up one of the wreaths. It was flawless each faux pine needle and plastic holly berry perfectly placed. It was also completely lifeless. "There's no soul in this, Noel. No story."

"It's consistent," he said, his own voice sounding hollow. "It's professional. It'll look perfect in the photos."

"People's memories aren't consistent," she shot back, dropping the wreath as if it had burned her. "Mrs. Gable's been hanging the same lopsided, handmade wreath on her door for thirty years. Her husband made it for her. Are you going to tell a widow her husband's memory isn't consistent with your brand identity?"

"Of course not," he said, his face flushing. "This is for the public spaces the storefronts…"

"The storefronts are people's lives, their dreams! Zara's yarn shop, my bakery they're extensions of us. You can't just slap a corporate logo on them and call it Christmas."

"I'm trying to save this town, Holly!" he said, frustration boiling over. "And I can't do that if I have to worry about every single lopsided wreath and handmade memory. There's a bigger picture here a hundred-thousand-dollar picture!"

"And what happens when the prize money's gone?" she demanded, stepping closer, her eyes blazing. "When the professional musicians have packed up and your perfectly consistent wreaths are back in their boxes? What'll be left of the town's soul then? You don't save a place by stripping it of everything that makes it unique."

Before he could answer, Zara came storming out of *The Tangled Skein*, a half-finished, brightly colored knitted scarf in her hands.

"Bishop!" she called sharply. "I just got your email. Are you seriously telling me I can't hang the knitted snowflakes the kids from the after-school program made for my window?"

"To maintain a cohesive aesthetic, all window displays should adhere to the approved guidelines," Noel recited, the corporate jargon sounding absurd on his tongue.

"It's a yarn shop!" Zara fumed. "It's supposed to look like it was decorated by a flock of color-blind, craft-obsessed sheep! That's the whole point that's my brand identity!"

She turned to Holly, then back to Noel, her eyes narrowing. "You know, for a guy who used to sketch the most imaginative, wonderful things, you've turned into a real killjoy. What happened to the boy who designed a gingerbread clock tower with licorice hands? He wouldn't be caught dead approving these boring, plastic wreaths."

Zara's words hit harder than Holly's. The gingerbread clock tower he hadn't thought of that sketch in fifteen years. It had been one of his favorites: whimsical, impractical, full of joy. A ghost of that boy looked out through Noel's eyes and was horrified by the man he'd become.

He had no answer. He could only stand there, caught between the logic of his plan and the truth of their accusations. He was winning the battle of logistics but losing the war for the town's heart and trampling all over Holly's in the process.

He watched as Holly put a comforting arm around Zara, the two of them a united front of fierce, creative resistance. They looked at him not as an old friend who had returned but as an invading force.

That evening, he sat alone in his sterile temporary office, the town map glowing under the desk lamp. The colored pins looked like a battle plan an occupation. He was doing everything right, everything his training and experience had taught him. He was building a better version of Christmas a version guaranteed to win.

But as he stared at the map, he didn't feel like a winner. He felt like a ghost haunting the edges of a life he used to know a life that was richer and more colorful before he streamlined it. He had come back to build their dream, but he'd brought the wrong set of blueprints.

Chapter 7

An Unscheduled Detour

For three days, a cold war raged on Main Street fought not with words but with a crippling, stubborn silence. Holly's original volunteer committee had staged a quiet mutiny. They still showed up at The Rolling Pin for coffee, their faces a mixture of loyalty and frustration, but they wouldn't touch a single one of Noel's "brand-cohesive" wreaths. They refused to implement his directives, leaving the identical boxes of decorations stacked like munitions on the pavement.

Noel, in turn, doubled down on his professional efficiency. He'd hired a small, bewildered crew of day laborers from a neighboring town to begin the work. The result was a jarring visual mismatch. On one side of the street, a shop window displayed a charming, slightly chaotic collection of handmade decorations from years past. On the other, a starkly perfect, uniformly lit display looked like a page torn from a catalog. The town didn't look festive; it looked like it was having an identity crisis. The heart and the head were not speaking, and the result was a disjointed, soulless mess.

The breaking point came in the form of a generator not just any generator, but a specific, high-amperage, whisper-quiet model Noel deemed essential for testing his new projection idea for Town Hall an idea developed in silent competition with Holly's. The local rental supply had nothing powerful enough.

The only one available for same-day pickup was at a specialty event-supply company in Rutland, an hour's drive away.

Holly was in the bakery, boxing up an order of morning buns, when Mayor Thompson cornered her. Noel stood a few feet behind him, looking uncomfortable, his arms crossed over his chest.

"Holly," the mayor began, his tone that of a desperate diplomat, "we have a problem. Noel needs to pick up a piece of vital equipment in Rutland. The project is at a complete standstill until he does."

"So he should go," Holly said, not looking at Noel. She folded the top of the pastry box with a sharp, definitive crease.

"Well, see, the thing is," the mayor continued, "you know those back roads better than anyone. And you know the owner, Mac. He'll give you a better deal. It would be a great help to the town budget if you went with him." He lowered his voice. "And besides, the two of you need to learn to work together. This silent treatment is tearing the committee apart. Please, Holly. As a personal favor to me for the good of the town."

It was a perfectly executed political maneuver. He'd made it impossible for her to refuse without seeming petty or obstructionist, like she was actively sabotaging the project. Her jaw tightened. "Fine," she clipped out. "For the good of the town."

The first twenty minutes in Noel's rented black SUV were the longest of Holly's life. The vehicle was aggressively new, with a sterile leather-and-plastic scent that was the polar opposite of her own flour-dusted car. It was a perfect metaphor for the man sitting beside her. He drove with quiet, focused competence that she found intensely irritating. The silence wasn't empty; it was heavy filled with the ghosts of their recent fight and the weight of their distant past.

She stared out the passenger window, watching the familiar Vermont landscape scroll by, cataloging every way he'd changed. The watch on his wrist probably cost more than her monthly mortgage payment. The lines around his eyes were new, etched there by stress and city living. The easy, open laughter she remembered was gone, replaced by this tense, controlled quiet.

He cleared his throat. "So… how are your parents?" he asked, the question sounding painfully stilted.

"They're fine," she replied, her gaze fixed on the passing trees. "They retired to Florida three years ago."

"Oh. Right. Dad mentioned that."

More silence. Holly felt a wild, hysterical urge to either scream or ask him about the projected ROI of this car ride.

Noel, for his part, felt like he was suffocating. He was acutely aware of her presence the faint, maddening scent of cinnamon and something uniquely Holly that clung to her clothes. He replayed their argument in the bakery on an endless loop. He wanted to apologize, to explain, but the corporate language he was fluent in was useless here. How did you file a prospectus for a decade of regret?

The sky, once a placid gray, began to darken with alarming speed. A few stray snowflakes appeared on the windshield, then a dozen, then a thousand. Within minutes, they were driving through a thick, swirling snow squall that blotted out the mountains and reduced visibility to near zero. The main highway became a slick, treacherous ribbon of gray.

"Turn here," Holly said suddenly, her voice sharp with authority. "Take the next exit Route 112. It's an old road, but the town crews keep it clearer than the state does."

Noel followed without question, turning onto a winding two-lane road that cut through a dense forest of pines. Here, the snow was even more beautiful, clinging to the heavy boughs of the evergreens. The world outside the car became a quiet, hushed wonderland a step back in time.

As they rounded a long, familiar curve, Holly felt her breath catch. Through the swirling snow, she saw an old, faded sign, its paint peeling but the words still legible: *Blackwood Pines. Cut Your Own.*

"I can't believe this place is still here," she whispered, more to herself than to him.

Noel's head turned toward the sign, his knuckles white on the steering wheel. "Blackwood Pines," he repeated, the name sounding foreign on his tongue. "Remember the time you tried to carry a tree that was twice your size?"

A small, unwilling smile touched Holly's lips. "You're one to talk. You got stuck in the netting machine, and Mr. Blackwood had to cut you out."

A ghost of his old, easy laugh surfaced a sound so unexpected it made Holly's heart ache. "I'd forgotten about that."

And just as the shared memory created the first fragile thaw between them, the engine sputtered. It coughed once, twice, then died with a final, definitive silence. The sleek, modern SUV drifted to a quiet halt on the side of the road.

"No," Noel muttered, turning the key. The engine only clicked a pathetic, futile sound against the hiss of falling snow.

"No, no, no. It's a rental. It's brand-new." He tried again. Click. Silence.

Holly looked out the window. The snow was coming down harder now. They were miles from the nearest town. And, inevitably, her phone had no signal. "Of course," she muttered.

Noel checked his. Nothing. "Okay," he said, his voice all business again. "We stay in the car and wait for a plow."

"The plows won't come down this far until the main roads are clear. That could be hours," Holly countered, her practical, small-town instincts kicking in. "And it's getting colder. We can't just sit here." Her eyes scanned the landscape. There was only one option. "The old sorting barn," she said, pointing through the trees. "At the farm. It's only a quarter-mile walk. At least it's shelter."

The barn was a time capsule. The massive sliding door groaned open on rusty rollers, revealing a cavernous space that smelled of old pine, dust, and cold earth. Sunlight filtered through grimy windows, illuminating dust motes dancing in the air. In one corner stood a pot-bellied stove; in another, a collection of antique sleighs sat under thick canvas tarps. It was a place steeped in the ghosts of Christmases past.

"We need to get a fire going," Noel said, his voice echoing in the vast space. His city coat looked inadequate now. He was shivering slightly.

For the first time since he'd returned, they worked together. It was an unspoken, instinctive collaboration. He, with his engineer's mind, checked the stovepipe and flue for blockages. She, with her country know-how, knew exactly where to find the driest kindling the old wooden tree stands stacked in a corner. They didn't speak much, but their movements were efficient and complementary. He broke up larger pieces of wood while she arranged the kindling in the stove.

When he finally struck a match and the kindling caught, casting a warm, flickering glow, they both exhaled in relief. They pulled an old wooden bench closer and huddled near the growing warmth.

"I really thought you were going to get frostbite that time you fell in Miller's Pond," Holly said into the comfortable silence, her voice soft.

Noel looked at her, his face illuminated by the firelight. The corporate architect was gone, and for a moment, he was just a boy from Evergreen Hollow again. "You were the one who pulled me out. You were surprisingly strong."

"I was running on pure adrenaline and terror," she admitted. "You were an idiot."

"I was," he agreed, a genuine smile reaching his eyes. "I was trying to impress you."

The admission hung in the warm air between them. They sat in silence for a long time, watching the fire dance and the snow fall in thick, quiet sheets outside the barn door. The anger and tension of the last few days seemed to belong to another world. Here, in this forgotten place, they weren't adversaries. They were just two people who shared a history, seeking warmth from the same fire.

"Holly," Noel said, his voice low. He didn't look at her, his gaze fixed on the flames. "About the meeting and the things I said in the bakery. I was an ass." He finally turned to her, his eyes filled with a sincerity she hadn't seen since he came back. "I came in too hot. I bulldozed you and your plan. I'm sorry."

The apology was simple, direct, and utterly disarming. Holly felt the tight knot of anger in her chest begin to loosen. "I know you think you're helping," she conceded softly. "It's just… this town, this contest it's personal for me. Every part of it is personal. And when you came in with your talk of ROI and branding, it felt like you were trying to erase the people, the memories."

"I see things in terms of systems and structures," he explained. "It's how I'm trained to think. I look at a problem and find the most efficient solution. I didn't stop to think about… the heart."

"The heart is the only thing we have left," she whispered.

Just as their fragile truce settled, a new sound cut through the quiet the low rumble of an old pickup truck. A moment later, a grizzled old man with a face like a roadmap and kind eyes appeared in the doorway. It was Silas Hemlock's older brother, Jed, the farm's caretaker for as long as either of them could remember.

"Well, I'll be," Jed said, his voice a gravelly rumble. "Figured I'd find someone in here. Saw the car down the road. Battery's dead as a doornail happens in these sudden freezes." He squinted. "Holly Sutton. And Noel Bishop? Haven't seen you in a dog's age. You two get in the truck. I'll give you a lift back to town."

The ride back in Jed's ancient, heater-blasting Ford was nothing like the ride out. The silence was no longer tense or angry it was thoughtful. Restorative. They sat on opposite sides of the bench seat, two separate people again, but the chasm between them had narrowed. The war wasn't over, but for the first time, there was the possibility of a ceasefire.

When Jed's truck rumbled back onto Main Street, the town's Christmas lights were flickering on in the late-afternoon gloom. It was a chaotic, jarring sight. On one side of the street, a warm, slightly messy glow emanated from the windows Holly's team had decorated. On the other, the cold, perfect, uniform light of Noel's directives shone with detached precision.

Holly and Noel both stared out the windshield at the visual representation of their conflict. For the first time since he'd returned, they saw the exact same thing a beautiful, heartfelt, chaotic mess. A project that was half head, half heart, and a town caught in the middle.

The truce they'd found in the quiet, snow-covered barn was over. Now, they had to figure out how to make it survive in the real world.

Chapter 8

Stranded In The Snow

The fragile truce forged in the firelight of the old barn did not survive the harsh, fluorescent reality of the Town Hall. Jed's truck had barely rumbled out of sight before Noel's phone began to buzz with a relentless, demanding rhythm. It was the lighting vendor, the string quartet confirming their schedule, and an increasingly irate Frank Henderson demanding a progress report. The corporate world, with its deadlines and deliverables, had found him again.

Holly, meanwhile, was greeted at the door of *The Rolling Pin* by a delegation of worried volunteers. Mrs. Gable fretted over the plastic wreaths. Silas Hemlock wanted to know if it was true the all-day bake sale had been canceled. They looked to her for reassurance, their faces reflecting the town's collective anxiety. The weight of their hopes and the responsibility of not letting them down settled on her shoulders like a heavy wool coat. The brief respite was over. They were back in their respective corners, the battle lines redrawn by the expectations of others.

For two days, they worked in a state of tense, unspoken détente. To his credit, Noel made an attempt at compromise. He sent out a revised directive a "Directive 2.0" that was a painfully transparent attempt to bridge the gap between their visions. It allowed for "one approved handmade item" per window display, alongside the corporate-approved décor. It reinstated the community bake sale but relegated it to a small tent at the far end of the square, away from the "main stage" of his *Tree Lighting Moment.*

The result was an even greater mess. Holly watched in dismay as her volunteers tried to follow the new rules, their efforts producing displays that were neither heartfelt nor professional. Zara's window now featured a single, lonely-looking knitted snowflake surrounded by a sea of perfectly uniform plastic candy canes. It looked less like a compromise and more like a hostage situation.

The town, which had been simmering with quiet resentment, began to boil over with open frustration. The volunteer committee fractured. Half, swayed by Frank Henderson's relentless pragmatism, reluctantly tried to implement Noel's plan. The other half, loyal to Holly, refused to participate in what they now called the "corporate Christmas takeover." Morale had hit rock bottom.

Holly found herself in an impossible position mediator, peacekeeper, therapist trying to soothe hurt feelings and negotiate micro-compromises over the placement of a garland or the wattage of a lightbulb. She felt like a UN envoy in a war fought with tinsel and glitter. She and Noel communicated only through terse, formal emails, each message a carefully worded negotiation. The warmth of the barn, the easy camaraderie of their shared past, felt like a distant dream.

The final straw was the town Christmas tree. A magnificent twenty-five-foot balsam fir, it had been donated by Blackwood Pines Farm a cherished annual tradition. Getting the tree from the farm to its place of honor in the town square was a massive, all-hands effort that officially marked the start of Evergreen Hollow's decorating season.

This year, however, Noel had deemed the traditional method a flatbed truck, a dozen volunteers, and a lot of hopeful shouting "unacceptably inefficient and a potential insurance liability." Without consulting Holly, he had hired a professional crane service from Burlington.

Holly was icing a batch of snowflake-shaped cookies when she saw it: a monstrous yellow crane rumbling down Main Street, its mechanical arm folded like a prehistoric insect. It was the most jarring, out-of-place sight she had ever seen in Evergreen Hollow. It felt like an invasion.

She dropped her piping bag, flour puffing into the air, and stormed outside. Noel was already there, clipboard in hand, directing the crane operator with crisp, efficient gestures.

"What is this?" Holly demanded, her voice shaking with anger. "What have you done?"

Noel turned, his expression hard with determination. "I've ensured the tree will be placed safely and precisely on its axis. We have a lighting grid to install. There's no room for error."

"This isn't an error it's a tradition!" she shot back, gesturing wildly. "For fifty years, this town has raised that tree together! It's a symbol! Mr. Hemlock's father used to drive the truck! The kids ride on the flatbed! You can't just... outsource our memories!"

"I'm trying to prevent a multi-ton tree from falling on your memories!" he retorted, his temper rising. "This is a professional operation now, not a high school pep rally!"

As they argued, a crowd began to gather her volunteers, his hired crew, curious shopkeepers. They were a spectacle, their private war turned public in the middle of Main Street.

"You don't get it," she said, lowering her voice to a fierce whisper. "You've been gone so long you don't even see it anymore. The point isn't the perfect, straight tree, Noel. The point is the *together.* The point is the shared effort, the story we tell afterwards. The point is the heart. And you're ripping the heart out of everything we do."

He opened his mouth to reply, but a shout from the crane operator cut him off. A sudden, violent gust of wind swept down from the mountains a harbinger of the coming storm. The massive tree, suspended twenty feet in the air by a single cable, began to sway, its huge branches groaning. The operator fought to control it, but the wind was too strong. With a sickening lurch, the tree swung sideways, its top branches snagging the town's main power line.

There was a shower of blue-white sparks, a sound like a giant firecracker, and then instantaneous darkness. Every light on Main Street, every light in the town, went out. A collective gasp rippled through the crowd as Evergreen Hollow was plunged into the eerie gray twilight of the approaching storm.

In the shocked silence that followed, one thing was clear: Noel's efficient, professional, streamlined plan had just blacked out the entire town.

Holly didn't hesitate. Years of small-town crisis management kicked in. "Everyone, stay calm!" she shouted, her voice cutting through the stunned quiet. "Go back to your shops and homes. Find flashlights, candles. We have a generator at the bakery anyone who needs warmth, come to *The Rolling Pin!*"

People began to move, murmuring anxiously. Holly turned to Noel. He stood frozen, clipboard dangling uselessly at his side, his face pale with shock. He stared at the darkened town, at the tangled mess he had caused. For the first time, the confident Chicago architect looked completely, utterly lost.

"The generator at the bakery can't power the whole town," Holly said, her anger replaced by steady practicality. "But the old backup generator at the mill can. It's ancient, but it's a diesel beast. It could get the town's core power back. The problem is, no one's started it in years. I'm not even sure it'll turn over in this cold."

Noel looked at her, a spark of focus returning the engineer awakening. "Diesel engines need glow plugs to warm up in the cold," he said, already thinking. "If the plugs are shot, we can bypass them. We'll need a direct heat source something powerful."

"I've got four commercial ovens and a half-dozen propane tanks at the bakery," Holly replied. They slipped into the same easy, collaborative rhythm they'd found in the barn. It was no longer about competing visions it was about saving their town.

"Okay," Noel said, a plan forming. "We need to get to the mill. We'll need a toolbox, heavy-duty jumper cables, and your propane. All of it."

The old mill stood at the edge of town, a hulking silhouette against the snow-dark sky. The wind howled through its broken windows, a lonely, mournful sound. The generator room was in the basement a cold, tomb-like space that reeked of rust and diesel. The generator itself was a monster: a massive green block of cast iron and steel from another era.

"This is it," Holly said, her flashlight beam slicing through the gloom.

For the next hour, they worked in frantic synchronization. Holly, familiar with the mill from childhood explorations, checked the old fuel lines for leaks. Noel, precise and methodical, threw open the generator's access panel, his hands moving like a surgeon's as he assessed the damage.

"The glow plugs are completely shot," he said, his breath misting in the freezing air. "We'll never get it to turn over on its own. We'll have to heat the intake manifold directly."

It was a desperate, long-shot plan. They set up the propane tanks, connecting them to the bakery's industrial torches the same ones Holly used to caramelize crème brûlées. While Noel bypassed the fried starter circuit, Holly aimed the roaring blue flames at the engine's frozen metal heart.

The noise was deafening the howl of the wind outside, the roar of the torches inside. In the flickering light, they made a strange pair: the small-town baker and the big-city architect, their faces smudged with grease and determination, working side by side to awaken a sleeping giant.

"Okay, I'm going to jump the solenoid!" Noel yelled over the roar. "When I signal, hit it with everything you've got!"

He raised his hand, then dropped it. Holly squeezed the triggers, sending a river of flame over the manifold. Noel touched the jumper cables to the contacts. The engine groaned, shuddered, and coughed a puff of black smoke.

"Again!" Noel shouted.

They tried again. Another groan. Another cough. Still nothing.

"It's no use," Holly said, her arms trembling from the effort. "It's too cold. It's seized."

"No," Noel growled. "One more time. For the good of the town, right?"

He looked at her, eyes blazing in the firelight. It wasn't a challenge it was a plea. A plea to believe. Not in his plan, but in *them*.

She took a deep breath, nodded, and aimed the torches once more.

"Now!" he yelled.

She gave it everything she had. Noel hit the contacts. The generator groaned, coughed and then, with a sound like thunder, roared to life. The massive engine caught, its rhythm uneven at first, then settling into a deep, steady rumble. A single bare lightbulb hanging from the ceiling flickered, then glowed with warm, golden light.

They stumbled back, ears ringing, faces flushed with heat and triumph. In the glow of that single bulb, they looked at each other grease-streaked, exhausted, exhilarated. They had done it.

And then, through the steady thrum of the engine, came a distant sound: a cheer rising from Main Street as the lights of Evergreen Hollow flickered back to life, one by one.

In that moment, standing in the warm, noisy, grease-scented heart of the old mill, there were no competing visions, no old resentments, no corporate directives only the shared, profound satisfaction of having weathered the storm together. Noel looked at Holly at the smudge of soot on her cheek and the fierce, triumphant light in her eyes and felt something he hadn't in a long time. It wasn't the pride of success.

It was the simple, undeniable warmth of coming home.

Chapter 9

The First Crack In The Ice

The walk back from the old mill was a surreal journey through a town reborn in light. The snow had softened to a gentle, quiet fall, the fat, lazy flakes glittering as they drifted through the golden cones of the newly reawakened streetlights. The cheer they'd heard from the basement of the mill had subsided into a low, happy hum that seemed to emanate from the very bones of the town. Windows that had been dark and forbidding were now warm, glowing squares of life. From inside houses and shops, Holly could hear the murmur of voices and the sound of radios clicking back on. They hadn't just restored power; they had restored the town's heartbeat.

Holly and Noel walked side by side, not touching, but the space between them no longer felt like a chasm. It was a space of shared accomplishment, filled with the lingering adrenaline of their success. The silence was different now, not the tense, angry quiet of the car ride, but a comfortable, weary one. Holly was acutely aware of the grease smudge on her own cheek and the matching one on Noel's jaw. It felt like a strange sort of battle paint, marking them as members of the same tribe.

"My grandmother always said this town had more ghosts than people," Holly said softly. "She would've loved this, a big, dramatic crisis followed by a miracle. It was her favorite kind of story."

"She would've been in her element," Noel agreed, his voice a low rumble. "She'd have been handing out hot chocolate and directing traffic, probably all at the same time." He paused, then added, "She was always... formidable."

"She was," Holly said with a fond smile. "She's the one who taught me how to handle a crisis. 'Panic is a wasted ingredient, Holly-berry,' she used to say. 'Figure out what needs doing, and then do it.'"

"That's exactly what you did," Noel said, his gaze finding hers in the soft glow of the streetlights. "You were incredible back there."

The compliment was so simple, so direct, and so free of corporate jargon that it caught Holly completely off guard. A warmth spread through her chest that had nothing to do with exertion.

"We were a good team," she admitted. The words felt both strange and completely natural.

As they rounded the corner onto Main Street, they were met with a scene of quiet, happy chaos. People were emerging from their homes, not with anxiety, but with a sense of communal relief. Mayor Thompson was the first to spot them, his round face breaking into a huge, beaming smile.

"There they are!" he boomed, his voice echoing down the street. "The heroes of the hour!"

Suddenly, they were surrounded. A spontaneous crowd of townspeople enveloped them, their faces glowing with gratitude. Mrs. Gable clasped Holly's greasy hand in both of hers, her eyes shining. Silas Hemlock gave Noel a gruff, approving nod which, for him, was the equivalent of a ticker-tape parade. Frank Henderson stood at the edge of the crowd, his arms crossed, his expression unreadable but notably lacking its usual cynical disapproval.

"We saw the lights come back on at the mill first," Zara said, pushing through the crowd and throwing an arm around Holly's shoulders. She glanced at the grease on Holly's face, then at the matching smudge on Noel's, and a slow, knowing grin spread across her face. "Looks like you two finally figured out how to collaborate."

The comment made them both flush, suddenly aware of their disheveled, united appearance. They were no longer two warring generals, they were a team, and the whole town was their audience.

"It was a temporary alliance to fight a common enemy," Holly said quickly, though there was no bite in her tone.

"The generator is a temporary fix," Noel clarified, his professional instincts kicking back in, but his voice was warmer than it had been in days. "The main power line will need a proper repair crew. But it'll hold for tonight."

After the crowd dispersed, with promises of free coffee for life and heartfelt thank-yous, Holly and Noel were left standing in front of *The Rolling Pin*. The warm light from its windows spilled out onto the snowy pavement like an invitation.

"Well," Holly said, breaking the quiet. "I don't know about you, but I could use something that isn't covered in diesel fumes."

"I think I have grease in my hair," Noel admitted, running a hand through it and grimacing.

"Come on," she said gently. "I'll make us some coffee. It's the least I can do."

Inside the bakery, the familiar warmth and the scent of cinnamon and sugar felt like a sanctuary after the cold, metallic chaos of the mill. The silence here was different too, a comfortable, domestic quiet filled with the gentle hum of the pastry case and the ticking of her grandmother's clock.

Holly moved with an easy, familiar grace behind the counter, her actions automatic. She pulled two clean mugs from a shelf, her hands steady now. Noel stood awkwardly in the middle of the customer area, looking too big and too formal for the cozy space, even in his grease-stained coat. He looked like a man who'd forgotten how to simply stand still.

"You can sit down, you know," Holly said, gesturing with her head toward the small table by the window, the one where she'd first sketched out her five-point plan.

He slid onto the stool, his movements hesitant, as if afraid he might break something. Holly brought over two steaming mugs, the dark, rich aroma of coffee filling the air. She sat opposite him, wrapping her cold hands around the warm ceramic.

For a long moment, they just sat there, sipping in silence, the warmth seeping into their bones. The adrenaline of the crisis was fading, leaving behind a profound, shared exhaustion.

"I never thanked you," Noel said quietly. "Back at the barn. For pulling me out of the pond."

Holly looked up, surprised. "We were ten, Noel. And I'm pretty sure I spent the next hour yelling at you for being a reckless idiot."

"You did," he confirmed with a small smile. "But you saved my life first. I always remembered that. You were always the one who ran toward the problem, not away from it." He took a sip of coffee, his gaze growing more serious. "I want you to know, Holly, I never meant for it to go this way. I didn't come back here to declare war on your traditions."

"Then what did you come back for?" she asked, her tone genuine, stripped of anger.

He stared down into his mug, as if the answer might be swirling in the dark liquid. "Honestly? I'm not entirely sure anymore. At first, it was simple, an easy PR win for my portfolio. A chance to see my parents. A way to... I don't know... show everyone I'd made something of myself." He looked up, his eyes soft with vulnerability. "But mostly, I think I was just tired. Tired of designing things that didn't matter. Those chrome reindeer you mentioned, you were right. They're soulless. I'm good at it, this corporate design world, but it feels like I'm building beautiful, empty boxes. I thought maybe if I came back here, I could remember what it felt like to build something with a heart."

His confession was so unexpected, so raw, that it knocked the breath out of her. It was the first time he'd spoken not as a consultant or an architect, but as a person. The ghost of the boy she used to know was suddenly sitting right across from her.

"The heart is still here," she said softly. "It's just... struggling to keep a steady rhythm." She took a breath, then added her own quiet truth. "And you were right, too. What you said in the bakery, about me hiding. A part of me has been. It's safe here. Familiar. But it's not the life I used to dream of. Looking at my grandmother's ledger, at all that red ink... it's terrifying. I've been so focused on keeping her legacy alive that I haven't let it grow. I've been afraid to take risks."

"The five-point plan isn't a risk," he said, his voice firm, his conviction rekindling her own. "It's brilliant. Especially Point Five, the projection. When you described it in the meeting, even when I was being a complete jerk, all I could think was… that's her. That's the designer I remember. The one who sees the magic."

The sincerity in his voice made her eyes sting. "And then you offered to replace it with a stock animation of snowflakes," she teased gently.

He winced. "Probably not my finest moment. In my world, that's what you do, you find the most efficient solution. You outsource. You streamline." He leaned forward, elbows on the table, expression earnest. "But what if we didn't? What if we actually did it, your idea, your story? The seed, the tree, the seasons. We could build it together. I could handle the technical side, the projectors, the rendering, the mapping. You'd be the creative director. The artist." He met her eyes. "What if we combined our two versions of the dream?"

There it was, not a compromise, not a concession, but a collaboration. A synthesis. It was the first real crack in the ice that had frozen between them for a decade. It was an offer to build something new, something that belonged to both of them.

Holly looked from Noel's hopeful, tired face to the chaotic but beautiful plans still taped to the wall. His logic, her heart. His technical skill, her creative vision. It was a terrifying, exhilarating thought. It was the only way forward.

"Okay, Bishop," she said, a slow smile spreading across her face, the first genuine one she'd given him since he'd arrived. "Let's build your bones and my magic."

He let out a breath he hadn't realized he'd been holding, a wide, relieved grin transforming his face and making him look years younger. It was the smile she remembered, the one that could make even the sourest shop owner happy.

Outside, the snow continued to fall, blanketing the town in a fresh, clean layer of white. It was a new beginning. The slate wasn't wiped clean, the ghosts and history were still there, but for the first time, it felt like they could build something new on top of it, together.

The ice had cracked, and through it, a fragile, hopeful green shoot was beginning to emerge.

Part 2

The Thaw

Chapter 10

A Tangle of Lights And Memories

The morning after the blackout was unnervingly quiet, as if the town itself were holding its breath. The fragile agreement Holly and Noel had reached in the warm, coffee-scented sanctuary of the bakery felt tenuous and dreamlike in the cold light of day. It was one thing to promise collaboration when fueled by adrenaline and exhaustion; it was another to actually make it work.

They met not in the contested territory of Town Hall or the emotionally charged space of the bakery, but on neutral ground the town square, midway between their two worlds. The offending crane was gone, and the magnificent balsam fir now stood straight and proud in its designated spot, a silent monument to their shared crisis and its resolution. A light, feathery snow was falling, dusting their shoulders and muffling the sounds of the morning.

"So," Holly began, pulling her gloves tighter, her breath forming a white cloud in the air. "Bones and magic."

"Bones and magic," Noel agreed, a small, tentative smile on his face. He held a tablet, but for once, it didn't look like a weapon. "I spent most of the night reworking the master plan. Trying to… integrate."

He showed her the screen. It was a digital schematic of the town, but it looked different now. He had taken her five points and given them structure a framework. He had overlaid her handwritten, heart-driven ideas with his own clean, logical lines. He'd calculated power requirements for the Memory Lane Project, created a 3D rendering of the Community Canvas on Henderson's wall, and mapped out a feasible timeline for the Evergreen Gala that even accounted for volunteer hours. And there, in the center of it all, was a placeholder for *Point Five: The Sutton Projection,* complete with a detailed list of the technical specifications they would need. He hadn't replaced her ideas; he had built scaffolding around them.

"It's…" Holly was momentarily speechless. "It's organized."

"It's a start," he said. "It's the bones. Now we need the magic."

"And the magic," she said with a sigh, "is currently collecting dust in the basement of the community hall."

Which is how they found themselves, an hour later, standing before a heavy oak door with a peeling sign that read *Storage.* The air that wafted out as Noel pulled the door open was a thick, cloying cocktail of mothballs, decaying paper, and the faint, ghostly scent of pine needles from half a century of Christmases past. The basement was a vast, dimly lit cavern a catacomb of forgotten festive cheer. Cardboard boxes, some so old they were sagging under their own weight, were stacked in precarious towers. Ancient, life-sized nativity figures stared out from under dusty tarps, their painted eyes wide and accusing.

"My God," Noel whispered, his voice echoing in the gloom. "It's a Christmas crypt."

"Welcome to my life for the past month," Holly said, flicking on a string of bare overhead bulbs that cast more shadows than light. "Somewhere in this… archaeological dig… are the decorations that represent the collective soul of Evergreen Hollow."

Their first official act of collaboration was to be an inventory. Their mission: to sort the salvageable from the sentimental junk, to figure out what parts of the town's past could be woven into its new, unified future.

They started on opposite sides of the room an unspoken agreement to maintain a safe distance. The initial silence was thick with awkwardness. The only sounds were the scraping of boxes and the rustle of brittle, ancient tinsel. But the basement was a treasure trove of triggers a library of shared history.

"No way," Noel said, his voice filled with delighted disbelief. He pulled a strange, lumpy object from a box. It was a papier-mâché angel, its halo bent, one wing torn, its face painted with a garishly cheerful, slightly demented smile. "It's the Henderson Angel. I thought this thing was destroyed in the Great Pageant Fire of '98."

Holly looked over, a genuine laugh bubbling up inside her. "Oh, my God. Frank Henderson's third-grade art project. His mother insisted it be the star on the town tree for a decade. It was hideous."

"It was a masterpiece of abstract horror," Noel agreed, a wide grin spreading across his face. "Remember when its head fell off mid-carol and almost took out the mayor?"

"I thought Mrs. Gable was going to have a heart attack," Holly laughed, the sound bright and clear in the dusty room.

The shared memory broke the tension. The silence that followed was lighter, filled with the warmth of their laughter. The first knot had been untangled.

They moved closer, tackling a section of boxes together. Each object they unwrapped from its yellowed newspaper cocoon was a story: a set of hand-carved wooden reindeer they both remembered from the library display; a box of delicate German glass ornaments that had once belonged to the town's founding family. They were untangling more than just decorations they were untangling the web of their own childhoods, realizing how deeply intertwined they were.

"This was my favorite," Holly said softly. She held up a small, surprisingly heavy ornament shaped like a tiny, detailed replica of *The Rolling Pin.* "My grandmother had it made the year she paid off the mortgage. She said it was to remind her that even the biggest dreams are built out of small, solid things."

Noel took it from her, his fingers brushing hers. The touch was brief, accidental, but it sent a jolt of static electricity through the space between them. He turned the little bakery over in his hands, admiring the craftsmanship. "She was an amazing woman," he said quietly. "She always made me feel like whatever crazy idea I had was possible."

"She had a gift for that," Holly agreed.

And then they found it. Tucked away in the far corner, a monstrous, looming shape under a heavy canvas tarp. It was the legendary Great Tangle a single, continuous strand of old-fashioned C9 Christmas lights rumored to be over a thousand feet long. For generations, volunteers had tried to unravel it, and for generations, they had failed, eventually giving up and shoving it back into its corner.

"The beast," Holly breathed, awe in her voice.

"I thought it was a myth," Noel said, pulling back the tarp. It was worse than he could have imagined a giant, multicolored knot of wire and glass, a Gordian Knot of festive frustration.

"There's no way," he started to say, but then he saw the look on Holly's face. It was a look of pure, stubborn determination.

"We have to try," she said. "These are the lights for the big tree. They have those old, oversized bulbs. They give off a different kind of glow a warmer light. It's… important."

And so, the real work began. They laid the massive knot out on the dusty concrete floor and each took an end. What followed was a slow, painstaking process a four-handed puzzle that required constant communication and cooperation.

"Okay, I'm going to feed my end under this green loop," he said, his voice focused.

"Wait, no, if you do that, you'll tighten the knot over here," she countered, pointing. "You need to go over it. Pass it to me."

They fell into a rhythm: pass and pull, duck and weave. The task forced them into a proximity that was both awkward and strangely intimate. They were often kneeling face-to-face, their heads close together as they studied a particularly stubborn section of the knot. Their hands brushed constantly. At one point, to get a better angle, Noel had to lean over her, his arm bracing him on the floor next to her shoulder. Holly froze, her breath catching in her throat. She could smell the faint, clean scent of his soap mixed with the dust of the basement. The world seemed to shrink to the small, charged space between them. He pulled back quickly, a flush creeping up his neck.

As they worked, they talked. The memories, stirred by the objects around them, began to flow freely. They talked about Mr. Blackwood's ancient, grumpy dog, about the terrible school plays they'd been in, about the time they'd tried to build a raft to sail on Miller's Pond and it had sunk in under a foot of water. They laughed and teased each other, the years of silence and anger melting away with every knot they undid.

They were untangling far more than a string of lights they were untangling years of misunderstanding, the pain of their separation. With every freed loop of wire, they were loosening the tight, painful knot of their shared history.

"I think," Noel said, his voice full of triumphant weariness after what felt like hours, "I think this is the last one."

He held up one end; she held up the other. Between them lay a single, impossibly long, gloriously untangled string of Christmas lights. It snaked across the entire length of the basement floor, a colorful, dormant river.

"We did it," Holly said, a wide, unbelieving smile on her face. She looked at him, her eyes shining in the dim light, and saw her own triumphant exhaustion reflected back at her.

"Let's see if the old beast still has any life in it," Noel said, his smile matching hers.

He found the plug and traced the wire to a nearby outlet. "Ready?" he asked.

She nodded.

He plugged it in. For a moment, nothing happened. Then, one by one, the old, oversized bulbs flickered to life a soft red, a deep blue, a warm amber, a vibrant green. The light they cast was just as Holly remembered: a soft, magical glow that pushed back the shadows and transformed the dusty, forgotten crypt into an enchanted grotto.

The warm, colorful light painted their faces, chasing away the weariness. They stood in the middle of the glowing labyrinth they had created, the air around them humming with the gentle energy of the ancient bulbs. The silence returned, but this time, it was filled with something new. The ghosts in the basement were no longer haunting them they were celebrating with them.

Noel looked at Holly really looked at her not as a problem to be solved or an adversary to defeat, but as the girl he had spent a decade trying, and failing, to forget. He saw the flicker of the same emotion in her eyes: recognition, remembering. The space between them, once charged with static and anger, was now filled with a different, more potent kind of electricity. It would have been the easiest thing in the world to close the distance between them.

But it was too soon. The ice had cracked, but the ground was not yet solid beneath their feet. Instead of stepping closer, he just held her gaze a silent acknowledgment of the moment passing between them.

"The magic," he said, his voice barely a whisper.

"The bones," she whispered back.

They emerged from the basement an hour later, blinking in the bright afternoon light, their faces smudged with dust, their clothes smelling of mothballs, but their steps were light. Zara was just closing up her shop and saw them come out of the community hall together. She watched as they stood for a moment, not talking, just looking at the great, untangled string of lights they had coiled up a trophy from their shared battle. A slow, hopeful smile spread across her face.

The great tangle was finally undone. The thaw was no longer a fragile crack in the ice it was the steady, unmistakable flow of a river beginning to find its way back to the sea.

Chapter 11

Blueprints And Buttercream

The success in the basement had shifted something fundamental in the town's atmosphere. The quiet mutiny was over, replaced by a cautious but palpable buzz of new energy. When Holly walked down Main Street now, people no longer looked at her with worried, questioning eyes; they looked at her with a glimmer of hope. The sight of her and Noel emerging from the community hall dusty and triumphant had been a more powerful message than any directive or town meeting. It was proof that a truce had been called, that the two warring sides of Evergreen Hollow's future were finally working together.

Their dynamic had settled into a state of careful, awkward politeness. They were partners now a fact they both acknowledged with a kind of terrified reverence. But their collaboration so far had been born of crisis first the blackout, then the Great Tangle. Now, they had to learn how to work together by choice, to build something new from a place of calm intention.

Noel's temporary office in the vacant storefront with its folding table and harsh fluorescent lighting felt entirely wrong for this new phase. It was a place for corporate takeovers, not for nurturing a fragile, budding partnership.

It was Holly who made the first move, a deliberate peace offering. She found him there on a Tuesday evening, hunched over his tablet, the stark loneliness of the room making him look smaller than he was.

"You can't possibly be creative in here," she said, making him jump. "It's like a room where dreams go to die."

He looked up, a weary smile tugging at his lips. "It's efficient."

"It's depressing," she countered. "Listen, the bakery's closed for the night. The big oak table in the back is free. It's got better light. And… I can make hot chocolate."

It was more than an invitation; it was an act of trust. She was letting him into her space her home, the heart of her world. Noel understood the significance immediately.

"I'd like that," he said, his voice softer than she'd ever heard it. "I'd like that a lot."

And so, the command center for *The Sutton Projection* moved to The Rolling Pin.

The sight of Noel setting up his sleek, high-tech equipment on the ancient, flour-dusted oak table was a study in contrasts. His glowing tablet, with its clean lines and cool blue light, sat beside her smudged charcoal sketches on thick parchment paper. His precise, metal architectural rulers lay next to a chipped ceramic jar full of pens and stray whisks. The air was a rich, warm blend of her world buttercream, cinnamon, yeast and his the faint, sterile electronic hum of his projector and the sharp scent of ink from his plotter pens. It was the physical manifestation of their new mission: to find harmony between blueprints and buttercream.

"Alright," Noel said, his initial awkwardness giving way to familiar professional energy as he connected a portable projector to his tablet. "Let's start with the bones."

He aimed the projector at the large blank wall behind the table, and a wireframe grid of the Town Hall's façade appeared, floating in the warm, dim light of the bakery. It was a ghostly, skeletal image of the familiar landmark.

"This is the challenge," he explained, his voice filled with a genuine passion Holly hadn't heard before. He was in his element now not as a corporate consultant, but as a designer. "The building isn't a flat screen. It has texture. The stone façade, the deep-set windows, the cornices… they all warp the projected image. We have to map the animation to the building's specific architecture, pixel by pixel. Otherwise, it'll look distorted, amateurish."

He was teaching her, she realized not dictating or dismissing, but sharing his world and his knowledge. He showed her how the software accounted for the depth of a window frame, how he could program the light to make it seem as though it were emanating from the stone itself. She watched, fascinated, as he manipulated the complex 3D model, his fingers dancing across the screen. He was an artist just a different kind. His medium was light and logic.

"Okay," she said after a while, her mind buzzing with new understanding. "I see the bones. Now for the magic."

She unrolled a massive sheet of paper covered in her own sketches the storyboard for their story in light. She talked him through the emotional arc she envisioned, her language a world away from his technical precision.

"It has to start small," she explained, tracing a drawing of a single glowing seed. "Almost imperceptibly. We want people to wonder if they're even seeing it at first. Then the first shoot shouldn't just appear it needs to unfurl, like it's taking a deep breath."

She spoke about the movement, the feeling, the pacing. She described how the branches of the growing evergreen should spread not with mechanical smoothness, but with a slight, organic hesitation. How the summer leaves should be a deep, vibrant green that felt alive with sunlight, and how the autumn colors should fade not abruptly but gently like a watercolor painting bleeding at the edges.

Noel listened, his intense gaze fixed on her sketches. He didn't interrupt or mention render times or brand identity. He just absorbed her vision, his technical mind translating her poetry into practical code.

They hit their first real collaborative stride when they reached the transition from autumn to winter.

"This is the trickiest part, technically," Noel said, pointing to the wireframe on the wall. "Animating thousands of individual leaves falling, and then seamlessly transitioning to thousands of individual snowflakes... the processing power required is huge. It could look jerky, unnatural."

Holly barely heard his technical concerns. She was lost in the feeling of the story.

"But that's not how it happens, is it?" she said, thinking aloud. "In real life, you don't just watch the last leaf fall and then the first snowflake. There's that one day that grey, quiet day in between. The day that just feels like snow is coming."

She grabbed a piece of charcoal and a fresh sheet of paper. "What if we don't show the leaves falling at all?" she said, her hand moving quickly. "What if the vibrant autumn colors just... soften? They fade into muted browns and golds, and then the light itself seems to get colder, turning a soft, silvery grey. And then, out of that grey light, the first snowflake doesn't fall it just materializes. A single point of bright white light. Then another. And another. Until the whole building is glittering."

Noel stared at her sketch, then at the wireframe on the wall, then back at her drawing. A slow look of wonder spread across his face.

"That's… brilliant," he said, his voice full of genuine awe. "That's not a technical solution it's an emotional one. It's simpler, more powerful, and it would be a thousand times more beautiful to watch." He looked at her, his smile reaching deep into his eyes. "You see the magic."

In that moment, they weren't adversaries or even tentative partners. They were a team. The synergy between them was a palpable, creative force. He saw the structure, and she saw the soul, and together they were creating something neither could have made alone.

The hours melted away. They worked in a comfortable, focused rhythm, fueled by Holly's strong coffee and a plate of warm, gooey, fresh-from-the-oven chocolate chip cookies. Noel ate three, his eyes closing in blissful satisfaction. "My God," he murmured after the first bite. "I'd forgotten what real food tastes like."

It was a simple act her feeding him, him accepting but it felt like the mending of a deep, ancient rift.

He, in turn, opened up about his life in Chicago the crushing deadlines, the demanding clients, the loneliness of celebrating a successful project launch with takeout in his empty apartment.

"This," he said, gesturing around the warm, fragrant bakery at the beautiful mess of their combined work, "is the most creative, the most… real I've felt in years."

They finally cracked the last part of the animation the ending. The magnificent, fully grown evergreen, glittering with snow, would slowly dissolve not into darkness but into a constellation of tiny, star-like points of light. And then, one by one, those stars would gather in the center of the Town Hall's façade, forming a single, brilliant, pulsing star of hope.

"That's it," Holly whispered, her heart pounding with the thrill of creation. "That's the end of the story."

"It's perfect," Noel breathed.

They were both standing now, looking at the final sketch pinned to the wall, their shoulders almost touching. The projector cast a soft blue glow, illuminating the dust motes dancing in the air and the exhaustion and elation on their faces. The bakery was silent, save for the gentle ticking of the clock and the hum of the ovens. The air was thick with the scent of sugar, chocolate, and a decade of unspoken feelings.

He turned to her, his expression serious, his eyes searching hers. "Holly, I…"

She turned to him at the same time, ready to thank him, ready to say something anything to acknowledge the fragile, beautiful thing they were building together in the quiet of the night.

They were inches apart. So close she could see the flecks of silver in his gray eyes, so close she could feel the warmth radiating from his skin. The world narrowed to this single, breathless moment. The creative energy that had been flowing between them all night coalesced into a different kind of energy a powerful, magnetic pull that was both terrifying and inevitable. He leaned in, his gaze dropping to her lips. She felt herself leaning forward, her eyes fluttering shut

BEEP. BEEP. BEEP.

The sudden, jarring sound of the oven timer shattered the spell. They sprang apart like startled teenagers, their faces flushed. The timer, set hours ago for a batch of slow-proofing bread, was a shrill, unwelcome intrusion from the real world.

"The bread," Holly stammered, her heart hammering against her ribs. She fled to the ovens, her back to him, her hands trembling as she fumbled with the latch.

The moment was gone the fragile bubble popped. An awkward, vibrating silence filled the space that had, seconds before, been humming with unspoken promises.

After she'd pulled the loaves from the oven, the rich scent of baked bread filling the air, they both knew the night was over. The creative energy had been replaced by a romantic tension so thick it felt hard to breathe.

As Noel packed up his equipment, his movements were clumsy, his usual efficiency gone. He paused, looking at the beautiful mess on the great oak table his sleek tablet nestled against her smudged charcoal sketches, an empty, chocolate-stained mug sitting next to a complex lighting equation he'd jotted down on a napkin. A genuine, unguarded smile touched his lips.

"You know," he said, his voice a low, warm rumble that sent a shiver down her spine, "I think blueprints and buttercream might be my new favorite combination."

He shouldered his bag and headed for the door.

"Goodnight, Holly."

"Goodnight, Noel," she whispered to the empty space where he had been.

She was left alone in the fragrant silence of the bakery, her heart pounding a wild, frantic rhythm against her ribs. She raised a trembling hand to her lips the ghost of the moment, of the almost-kiss, still tingling on her skin. She looked at their combined work, at the story they had built together a story that was part him, part her, and wholly new.

The thaw was no longer just a thaw. It felt like the first warm, terrifyingly hopeful day of a long-awaited spring.

Chapter 12

The Grumpy Craftsman on Elm Street

The creative high from their late-night session in the bakery carried Holly and Noel through the next forty-eight hours. A new, invigorating energy pulsed through the project. Armed with a unified plan, they moved with a shared sense of purpose that was infectious. Volunteers, seeing Holly and Noel walking through town together, deep in conversation over sketches and printouts, felt the shift and returned to the project with renewed enthusiasm. The awkward, mismatched decorations began to come down, replaced by a cohesive vision that felt like the town only brighter.

Their biggest logistical hurdle, however, was Holly's Memory Lane Project. The idea was simple and powerful, but the execution was complex. They had selected twenty stunning, large-format photographs from the town's archives, each one a window into a bygone Christmas. To display them along the path to Town Hall, exposed to the harsh Vermont winter, they needed more than just picture frames they needed small, durable, beautifully crafted display cases, each with its own internal, low-wattage lighting system to protect the photos and make them glow. It was a project that required the skill of a cabinetmaker, the precision of an engineer, and the soul of an artist.

"There's only one person who can do this," Holly said with a sigh, staring at the ambitious blueprint Noel had drawn for the cases. They were sitting in *The Rolling Pin*, the morning rush just beginning to ebb.

"Who?" Noel asked, looking up from his tablet. "Is there a custom fabrication shop in Rutland?"

"Better," Holly said, a wry smile on her lips. "And worse. We have Arthur Vance."

Noel frowned, the name not ringing a bell. "And he is?"

Just then, Zara bustled in, shaking snow from her purple coat. "Did I hear you invoke the name of the Ghost of Christmas Curmudgeon?" she asked, grabbing a mug from under the counter and helping herself to coffee. "You're not seriously thinking of asking Arthur Vance for help, are you?"

"We need custom-built, weatherproof, illuminated display frames," Holly explained. "Twenty of them. In three weeks. Who else is there?"

Zara shuddered theatrically. "You'd have better luck asking a badger to knit you a sweater. Arthur Vance hasn't participated in a town event since the council denied his petition to restore the old millworks back in '03. He said, and I quote, 'This town has chosen progress over history, so it can damn well rot in its own cheaply constructed future.' He's been happily holding that grudge ever since."

"He sounds charming," Noel said dryly.

"He's a master craftsman," Holly countered, a note of respect in her voice. "His work is… perfect. He's the only one who can do this right. His workshop is on Elm Street. He lives there. He never leaves." She looked at Noel, her expression a mixture of determination and dread. "We have to try."

Arthur Vance's workshop was less a building and more a monument to stubborn, solitary craftsmanship. It was an old, beautifully maintained timber-frame barn that stood apart from the other houses on Elm Street, smelling richly of cedar sawdust, linseed oil, and time. As they approached, the only sound was the rhythmic scrape of a hand plane against wood.

Holly took a deep breath before knocking on the massive, heavy oak door. The scraping stopped. A moment later, the door creaked open a few inches, and a pair of sharp, suspicious blue eyes peered out at them. Arthur Vance looked exactly as Holly had always pictured him: a man in his late sixties with a face that seemed to have been hewn from a block of stubborn oak, all sharp angles and deep-set lines. A fine layer of sawdust covered his flannel shirt and silver hair.

"We're closed," he grumbled, his voice a low, gravelly rasp. He began to shut the door.

"Mr. Vance, wait," Holly said quickly. "I'm Holly Sutton, from *The Rolling Pin.* My grandmother was Eleanor Sutton."

The door stopped closing. Arthur's gaze softened for a fraction of a second. "Eleanor was a good woman. She made a proper sourdough. Not like the fluffy nonsense they sell in supermarkets." He looked from Holly to Noel, his eyes narrowing again at the sight of Noel's city coat and expensive boots. "What do you want?"

"We came to ask for your help," Holly began, launching into the heartfelt, community-driven appeal she had rehearsed. She spoke of the contest, the importance of honoring the town's history, and the emotional power of the archival photos. She painted a picture of families walking the path to Town Hall, reconnecting with their shared past, their faces glowing in the light of the displays.

Arthur Vance listened, his expression unchanging, his arms crossed over his chest. When she finished, he just snorted, a dry, dismissive sound.

"Hope and glitter," he said, his voice dripping with disdain. "That's all you're selling. The council lets the foundation of the covered bridge rot for a decade, but they want to spend money on pretty pictures. You think a few lit-up photographs are going to fix the cracks in this town? The cracks go all the way to the foundation." He shook his head. "I don't build temporary, sentimental nonsense. I build things to last. The answer is no." He started to close the door again.

"Wait," Noel said, his voice calm but firm. He stepped forward, his eyes not on Arthur's grumpy face but on the workshop visible behind him. "Is that an Adirondack guide boat you're restoring?"

Arthur paused, surprised by the specific, knowledgeable question. "What's it to you?"

"The ribbing," Noel said, craning his neck to see better. "It's steam-bent white oak, isn't it? The curves are perfect. It's almost impossible to get that kind of uniform bend without fracturing the grain. Your setup must be impeccable."

Holly watched, amazed, as Arthur's entire posture shifted. The grumpy gatekeeper was replaced by the proud craftsman. He opened the door wider a grudging invitation into his world. "Took me years to perfect my steam box," he admitted, a note of pride in his gravelly voice. "You know anything about woodworking?"

"A bit," Noel said, stepping into the magnificent, cluttered space. "My degree is in architecture. I focused on structural design. I spent more time with wood stress-load tables than I did with people." He ran a hand reverently over a massive raw slab of cherry wood leaning against a wall. "This is beautiful. Where did you source it?"

For the next ten minutes, Holly was a silent observer as two masters of their craft spoke a language she didn't fully understand. They talked of dovetail joints versus mortise and tenon, of the benefits of tung oil versus polyurethane, and of the challenges of working with burled maple. Noel wasn't flattering him; he was engaging him, showing a deep, genuine respect for the skill and knowledge that filled the workshop. He wasn't the corporate consultant anymore he was a builder, a designer, a man who understood the profound satisfaction of making something real and lasting with his own two hands. He had found common ground, a shared language of structure and material.

Finally, when a comfortable, mutual respect had settled in the sawdust-filled air, Noel gestured to the roll of blueprints under his arm. "Mr. Vance, the project Holly mentioned it's not just sentimental. It's structural."

He unrolled the blueprint for the display cases on a clear workbench. It was a thing of beauty in its own right: a professional, detailed architectural drawing showing every measurement, join, and material specification. It even included a small, concealed ventilation system to prevent condensation from the internal lighting and specified the exact type of marine-grade sealant needed to make the oak frames impervious to a Vermont winter.

Arthur Vance leaned over the blueprint, his sharp eyes scanning every detail. He was silent for a long time, tracing the lines with a calloused finger. He let out a low whistle. "This is a proper design," he grumbled the words a high form of praise.

"You accounted for wood expansion in freezing temperatures. Nobody ever thinks of that." He looked from the blueprint to Noel, his expression one of grudging admiration. "You designed this?"

"I did," Noel said. "The bones of it, anyway."

"And I designed the magic," Holly said softly, stepping forward. She carefully placed one of the archival photographs on the workbench next to the blueprint. It was a stunning black-and-white image from the 1950s, showing a group of proud, smiling men in heavy wool coats standing before the then-newly completed Town Hall clocktower. In the front row, a handsome young man with a familiar, stubborn set of eyes was laughing.

Arthur Vance froze. He stared at the photograph, his gruff façade crumbling away to reveal a sudden, profound vulnerability. "That's my father," he whispered, his voice thick with emotion Holly had never imagined him capable of. "He helped build that clocktower. He carved the original oak casings for the clockworks."

"I know," Holly said gently. "This is the photo we want to put in the first frame your frame. We wanted the grain of your oak to honor the work he did."

It was the perfect one-two punch. Noel had appealed to his head his craft, his professionalism. Holly had appealed to his heart his history, his legacy. The grumpy craftsman on Elm Street didn't stand a chance.

Arthur stared at the photograph of his father for a long moment, then looked back at the flawless blueprint. He cleared his throat, the gruff mask sliding mostly back into place. "It's a rush job," he muttered, though the words lacked their earlier bite. "It'll cost you. I use premium-grade materials. No particle board nonsense in my shop."

"We wouldn't have it any other way," Noel said, a slow smile spreading across his face.

"Fine," Arthur sighed, turning away to hide the moisture that had gathered in his eyes. "I'll do it. But don't expect me to be hanging any tinsel. I'm building the frames that's it. And I expect to be paid on time."

"You will be," Holly promised, her heart soaring.

They left the workshop and walked out into the crisp, late afternoon air, a shared sense of giddy triumph warming them against the cold. The setting sun cast long, blue shadows down Elm Street.

"'You know anything about woodworking?'" Holly said, teasingly imitating Noel's earlier tone. "Where did that come from?"

"My grandfather was a cabinetmaker," Noel admitted, a nostalgic look on his face. "I spent summers in his workshop. It smells the same as Arthur's sawdust and turpentine. Funny, I haven't thought about that in years."

"Well, your grandfather would be proud," she said sincerely. "You were incredible in there. Your blueprints alone wouldn't have been enough."

"And your heartfelt plea wouldn't have gotten us past the front door," he countered, his eyes crinkling in a smile. "But the photo... Holly, that was the masterstroke."

"Bones and magic," she said, bumping her shoulder gently against his.

They walked in comfortable silence for a moment, the victory settling around them. They looked back and saw the warm, yellow light of the workshop glowing in the twilight. Through the window, they could see the silhouette of Arthur Vance, his head bent, already clearing a space on his main workbench and unrolling Noel's blueprint to study it under the light.

They had done more than just secure a vendor they had convinced a stubborn old man to believe in a town he thought had forgotten him. They had brought a ghost of Christmas past back into the fold. They looked at each other, a shared, unspoken understanding passing between them. Their partnership wasn't just about a contest anymore. It was about mending things that had been broken for a very long time.

Chapter 13

Echoes on The Old Town Bridge

The victory with Arthur Vance felt like a turning point. It was the first time they had faced an external obstacle as a united front, and their success had solidified their fragile partnership into something sturdy and real. A new, easy camaraderie settled between them. The awkward silences were replaced by comfortable quiet, the stilted questions by genuine conversation. They found themselves talking not just about the contest, but about everything and nothing the best way to roast a chicken, the terrible music of their high school years, the quiet, unspoken grief of watching a beloved town slowly fade.

Their next major task was the Old Town Bridge. It was the postcard image of Evergreen Hollow a classic covered bridge that spanned the semi-frozen Blackwood River, its weathered timber a testament to a century of endurance. In Holly's plan, the bridge was to be a centerpiece, a gateway to the festive heart of the town, draped in garlands and glowing with warm, golden lights.

They arrived in the late afternoon as the winter sun began its descent, casting a pale, golden light that made the snow-covered riverbanks sparkle. The air was still and cold, the only sounds the crunch of their boots on packed snow and the faint gurgle of the river moving beneath a thin sheet of ice.

They began, as they often did now, with their distinct but complementary roles. Noel, the architect, was all about the bones. He moved with focused intensity, inspecting the massive timber trusses, tapping on support beams, and using a laser measure for precise dimensions. He spoke of load-bearing capacity, weather-resistant junction boxes for the wiring, and the optimal placement for electrical connections to ensure a balanced power draw. He saw the bridge as a beautiful, complex structure that deserved to be respected and understood.

Holly, meanwhile, saw the magic. She walked the length of the bridge, her gaze drifting from the intricate latticework of the trusses to the way the afternoon light filtered through the gaps in the timbers, creating shifting patterns on the snow-dusted floorboards. She spoke of how the lights should feel like a warm, welcoming hug, and how the garlands should be woven with natural elements pinecones and dried berries gathered by the town's children. She saw the bridge not as a structure, but as a stage for a story.

"If we run the main power cable along this upper beam," Noel said, pointing upward, his voice echoing slightly in the enclosed space, "we can conceal it completely. Then we can drop connections at ten-foot intervals. It'll be a clean, safe, and efficient system."

"And at each drop," Holly added, coming to stand beside him, "we can hang a larger cluster of lights with a big, red velvet bow. That way, it looks intentional like a feature, not just a string of lights. It'll create a rhythm as you walk through."

"A rhythm," Noel mused, looking at her with a slow smile. "I like that. Structure and rhythm."

"Bones and magic," she replied, her own smile matching his.

They were so in sync, their two approaches meshing so perfectly, that it felt as if they had been working together their whole lives. The decade of silence and separation seemed like a strange, forgotten dream.

As Noel finished his final measurements, Holly wandered over to the large, open window on the side of the bridge the one that offered the most perfect view of the river and the snow-covered pines beyond. She ran her mittened hand along the thick, worn wooden railing, her fingers tracing the graffiti of generations. And then, her fingers stopped.

The carved letters were old, their edges softened by years of weather and touch, but they were still unmistakably theirs.

NB + HS

Enclosed in a slightly lopsided, heart-shaped box.

"Oh," she breathed, the sound small and fragile in the quiet air.

Noel heard the change in her voice and walked over, his boots echoing on the wooden floorboards. He looked at where her hand rested, and a sudden stillness came over him. He reached out, his bare fingers tracing the familiar lines of the letters he had carved with a pocketknife one cold October afternoon when they were sixteen.

"I can't believe this is still here," he said, his voice low and full of wonder. "I remember being so nervous your dad would see it and kill me for vandalizing town property."

"He did see it," Holly said, a soft, nostalgic laugh in her voice. "He just told me that if you were going to carve your initials somewhere, you'd better be sure you meant it." She looked up at him, her eyes searching his. "We meant it, didn't we?"

The question hung in the cold, still air between them. The professional façade, the careful partnership it all dissolved in the face of this simple, profound artifact of their shared past. They were no longer the consultant and the committee lead. They were just Noel and Holly, standing in the place where they had fallen in love.

"Yeah," he said, his voice thick with emotion. "We did."

The floodgates of memory opened. The echoes of the past, always whispering at the edges of their interactions, were suddenly shouting in the quiet of the bridge.

"This was our place," Holly said, her gaze drifting out over the river. "After our first real date at The Majestic… we walked here. I was so cold, and you gave me your coat, even though you were shivering."

"You were wearing that blue dress," he remembered instantly, his voice tinged with warmth. "And you had your hair up. I was terrified to even hold your hand." He looked down at the carved heart. "This is where I told you about my dream about wanting to be an architect. You were the first person I ever told."

"And this is where I showed you my first real sketchbook," she added softly. "You didn't laugh at my fantastical, impossible buildings. You told me I saw the world differently and that it was a gift."

The promises they had made to each other in this very spot seemed to hang in the air around them, visible in their breath.

The promise to build a future together, to cheer each other on, to always come back to this place. One of them had kept that promise. The other had not.

The weight of that unspoken truth settled between them, heavy and sorrowful.

"I was so focused on the blueprint, Holly," Noel said, finally giving voice to the regret that had haunted him. "I thought our dream was something I had to go away to build a tangible structure. I thought I had to construct the perfect, successful future before I could come back and present it to you. I didn't understand that for you, the dream was a living thing a garden you tended every day, right here." He shook his head, the self-reproach clear in his eyes. "I was so focused on building that future, I didn't realize I was bulldozing our past to make room for it."

Tears pricked at Holly's eyes for the boy he had been, for the man he had become, and for the years they had lost between. "And I was so focused on protecting the past," she admitted, her voice trembling slightly, "that I was terrified to even think about a different future. When you left, and everything here started to fall apart... holding on to what we had felt like the only solid thing in the world. I was afraid that if I let go, I'd have nothing left."

It was the most honest they had ever been with each other a mutual confession, a shared acceptance of their own fear and flawed logic. It wasn't absolution, but it was a kind of peace. The anger was gone, replaced by a deep, aching regret for the time they could never get back.

The sun had dipped below the mountains now, plunging the world into soft blue twilight. The first brilliant stars began to appear in the deep indigo sky. A light, magical snow started to fall again, the flakes drifting lazily into the quiet space of the bridge.

Noel reached out, his movements slow, hesitant. He gently tucked a stray strand of Holly's blonde hair, now dusted with snowflakes, behind her ear. His fingers were warm against her cold skin, and the simple, tender touch sent a shiver through her entire body.

"Holly," he whispered, his voice heavy with a decade of waiting.

He cupped her cheek, his thumb brushing her skin. She leaned into his touch, her eyes fluttering shut. The world seemed to melt away, leaving only the two of them suspended in time, in the quiet, snow-filled space of the bridge, surrounded by the echoes of their own history.

He leaned in slowly, giving her every chance to pull away. She didn't. She tilted her head up, her lips parting slightly. This was it the moment that had been building since he'd first walked back into her life, the moment she had been both dreading and longing for.

Just as their lips were about to meet, a deep, resonant sound rolled through the valley, pure and clear in the cold air.

Bong. Bong. Bong.

The old town clock chimed six times.

The sound familiar and constant as the river below broke the spell. They pulled back, their faces flushed, their breaths coming in ragged gasps. The moment was gone, lost to the relentless ticking of time the same clock that had been counting down the days of Holly's desperate miracle plan.

He dropped his hand, and the loss of his warmth felt like a physical ache. An awkward, charged silence fell between them.

"We should… finish up," Holly stammered, turning toward the now-dark river, her heart hammering against her ribs.

"Yeah," he said quietly. "The lights. We should… check the lights."

They finished their work in a haze of trembling awareness, their hands brushing occasionally each accidental touch feeling like a shout in the quiet.

They walked back to town in a new kind of silence. It wasn't angry, or awkward, or even comfortable. It was a silence that hummed with the powerful, unfulfilled energy of what had almost happened on the bridge. The echoes of the past had given way to a promise a question that now hung, unanswered, in the glittering winter air between them.

Chapter 14

An Almost-Kiss In The Glow

The days following their adventure on the Old Town Bridge were charged with a new, unspoken energy. The near-kiss had created a hum of electricity between Holly and Noel a constant awareness that made every shared glance, every accidental brush of hands, feel significant. They didn't talk about it. They couldn't. The moment had been too fragile, too burdened with a decade of complications to be dissected with clumsy words. So, they poured that energy, that humming, nervous tension, into their work.

And the work, for the first time, was thriving.

Their partnership had become the town's new engine. The volunteer committee, sensing the shift from civil war to true collaboration, was now fully engaged a small army fueled by Holly's seemingly endless supply of coffee and scones. They worked alongside the small professional crew Noel had hired, the initial suspicion between the two groups dissolving into surprising camaraderie. The townspeople, who had been watching the chaotic preparations with weary skepticism, began to feel something they hadn't in a long time: genuine excitement.

Their first major public test was the official lighting of the Old Town Bridge. It wasn't the grand Evergreen Gala, but a smaller, preliminary event a "First Look Friday" designed to showcase their progress and, more importantly, to prove to the town that their newfound unity could produce tangible, beautiful results.

The day of the lighting, the area around the bridge was a hive of controlled, happy chaos. It was the first time their "bones and magic" philosophy was on full public display. Noel, tablet in hand, moved with quiet, confident authority, directing final technical checks and ensuring every connection was secure, every spotlight perfectly angled. He spoke to the volunteers with newfound respect, answering their questions patiently, his corporate jargon replaced by the clear, simple language of collaboration.

Holly, meanwhile, was the heart of the operation. She moved through the crowd of volunteers, a thermos of hot cider in one hand, offering encouragement, tweaking garlands, and ensuring the natural, homespun elements weren't lost amid the technical precision. She was in her element her face flushed with a mixture of cold air, exertion, and pure, unfiltered joy.

Even Arthur Vance had made an appearance. He arrived in his old pickup truck to deliver the first four of his magnificent, handcrafted display frames for the Memory Lane project. He grumbled about the deadline and the cold, but Holly saw the deep, undeniable pride in his eyes as he and Noel carefully mounted them onto the bridge's interior walls. He lingered for a long time, watching the preparations a silent, grumpy, but undeniably present member of the community once more.

The only shadow on the otherwise perfect day was the arrival of Frank Henderson, his clipboard a veritable shield of skepticism. He marched onto the bridge, expression grim, and began a self-appointed "safety and budget inspection."

"This power draw seems excessive, Bishop," he said, peering at the main junction box. "Are you sure the town's grid can handle this? I don't want a repeat of that blackout fiasco."

"The total amperage is well within the grid's capacity," Noel replied calmly, tapping his tablet and showing Frank a complex-looking graph. "I've run the simulations. The blackout was caused by a direct short, not an overload. This system is independently circuited and fused. It's perfectly safe."

Frank grunted, unable to argue with the data. "And what about the volunteer hours? This is taking longer than projected. That means overtime for your hired crew, which wasn't in the approved budget."

Before Noel could respond, Holly stepped in her smile warm but her eyes firm. "Actually, Frank, we're ahead of schedule. The volunteers have been so amazing, they've handled all the garland and wreath placement, which means Noel's crew can finish the wiring an hour early. We'll be done well under budget." She gestured to a group of teenagers expertly weaving fresh pine boughs under Zara's watchful eye. "Turns out a little community spirit is incredibly efficient."

Defeated on both fronts, Frank could only offer a curt, dissatisfied nod and retreat. Noel caught Holly's eye over Henderson's departing shoulder and gave her a small, conspiratorial wink. She felt a giddy, triumphant laugh bubble up inside her. They were a team an unbeatable team.

As twilight began to bleed across the sky, painting the snow-covered landscape in shades of violet and rose, the town began to gather. They filled the riverbank, faces upturned and expectant, breath misting in the cold, crisp air. Holly and her team of volunteers served hot cider and her famous gingerbread cookies the ones with the smiling faces still intact. The atmosphere buzzed with nervous, hopeful energy. This was it. The moment of truth.

Mayor Thompson, beaming with pride, stood on a small, makeshift stage. "Friends! Neighbors!" he boomed, his voice full of emotion. "For the past few weeks, we've all been working toward a common goal. We've had... well, some different ideas about how to get there." A ripple of laughter ran through the crowd. "But tonight, we see what can happen when we combine the proud, heartfelt traditions of our past with the bright, innovative ideas of our future. And we have two people to thank for bringing those worlds together." He gestured toward them. "Holly Sutton and Noel Bishop!"

A wave of genuine applause swept through the crowd. Holly felt a blush rise up her neck. She looked at Noel, and he was already looking at her a shared, nervous excitement in his eyes.

"It is my honor," the mayor continued, "to ask the two of them to do the honors. Holly, Noel light it up!"

They walked together to the large, industrial control box. It felt strangely formal, like the final scene of a movie. Their hands one soft and mittened, the other bare and strong reached for the large, old-fashioned lever. They looked at each other, a silent question passing between them. Ready? She nodded.

Together, they pushed the lever down.

For a single, heart-stopping second, nothing happened. The crowd held a collective breath. And then, with a soft, satisfying hum, the bridge exploded with light.

It was breathtaking a perfect, harmonious fusion of both their visions. The warm, golden, nostalgic glow of the old-fashioned C9 bulbs was the dominant light, creating the welcoming, magical atmosphere Holly had dreamed of. But

Noel's invisible spotlights highlighted the bridge's magnificent trusses, giving it depth and grandeur. The lush green garlands were woven with bright red berries and pinecones gathered by Holly's volunteers, and at precise intervals, Arthur Vance's beautifully crafted frames glowed from within, the black-and-white photos of the town's history shining with a soft, reverent light.

It was bones and magic. It was structure and soul. It was perfect.

A collective gasp of wonder rose from the crowd, followed by a roar of cheers and applause that echoed through the quiet valley. People hugged, laughed, and pointed. Zara whooped with joy. Silas Hemlock actually smiled. Even Frank Henderson, standing at the back, looked grudgingly impressed. They had done it. They had won the town.

In the happy, celebratory chaos, as people surged forward to get a closer look, Holly and Noel found themselves drawn away from the crowd, pulled back toward the bridge itself. They stepped into the tunnel of golden light, the sounds of celebration fading, the world shrinking to just the two of them and the glow they had created.

They walked to the center of the bridge, stopping at the window with the carved initials. The light caught the snow falling outside, turning the flakes into a glittering cascade.

"We did it," Holly whispered, her voice full of awe.

"No," Noel said softly, turning to her. "We did it. Together."

The air between them, already charged from victory, thickened with something else entirely. The hum of the lights, the soft fall of snow, the distant cheers it all faded. He reached out and brushed a snowflake from her hair, his fingers lingering against her temple. His touch was warm, electric.

"Holly," he breathed, his gaze dropping to her lips.

This time, there was no hesitation. He leaned in, and she met him halfway.

The kiss wasn't sudden or fiery. It was slow, deep, and certain a homecoming. It was tender and tentative at first, a question asked and answered. Then, as a decade of unspoken feelings and longing rushed to the surface, it deepened. It tasted of cold winter air, of sweet gingerbread, of the unmistakable comfort of home. It was a kiss that said, *Oh, there you are. I've been looking for you.*

When they finally broke apart, breathless, their foreheads rested together. The golden glow of the bridge enveloped them in a private, magical world. The kiss had changed everything, and they both knew it. It had melted the fragile ice of their past, leaving them standing in the rushing, beautiful flood of the present.

He looked into her eyes, and she saw shock, wonder, and a hint of fear a perfect reflection of her own.

What now?

The question pulsed between them. There was no answer. They couldn't go back to being just partners. They weren't ready to be anything more. They stood in a new, undefined, electrifying space.

Slowly, they walked back toward the edge of the bridge and the sounds of celebration. They didn't rejoin the crowd. They stood at the periphery, watching the happy, illuminated faces of the townspeople they had helped save. They stood side by side, not touching, but connected by the powerful, undeniable truth of what had passed between them, their faces lit by the warm, steady glow of the bridge.

The project was a success. Their partnership was a success. But their story had just become infinitely more complicated.

Chapter 15

Pine Ridge Plays Dirty

The morning after the bridge lighting, Evergreen Hollow woke up to a town transformed. The success of *First Look Friday* had done more than just illuminate a landmark it had ignited a town-wide bonfire of hope. The air in The Rolling Pin was thick with it, an energy almost as intoxicating as the scent of fresh coffee and cinnamon rolls. People didn't just order their coffee; they lingered, talking excitedly, their voices buzzing with a civic pride that had been dormant for years.

For the first time, winning didn't feel like a desperate, far-fetched dream. It felt possible. It felt probable.

The atmosphere between Holly and Noel was equally transformed. The kiss had been a seismic event, shifting the very ground beneath their feet. When he walked into the bakery that morning, the awkwardness was there, but it was a sweet, humming tension not the brittle silence of before.

"Morning," he said, his smile a little shy, his eyes holding hers for a moment too long.

"Morning," she replied, her cheeks flushing as she handed him a coffee. "I was thinking… about last night."

"Me too," he murmured, his voice low, meant only for her even in the crowded bakery.

"We should probably talk about it," she said, her heart doing a nervous little flip.

"We definitely should," he agreed. He glanced around at the bustling room, then back at her. "But maybe after we've actually, you know, won this thing?"

A wave of relief washed over Holly. It was the perfect answer. It wasn't a dismissal it was a promise. A shared goal that put a protective bubble around the fragile, beautiful thing that had sparked to life between them in the golden glow of the bridge.

"Deal," she said with a genuine smile. "Partners first."

"Partners," he confirmed, and the simple word was loaded with new, unspoken meaning.

Their partnership was on full display all morning. They moved through the town as a single, efficient unit fielding questions from volunteers, coordinating with Arthur Vance on the next batch of frames, and finalizing the layout for the Evergreen Gala. The town saw them not as two separate leaders but as a team their combined energy a force of nature.

The attack came just before noon. It was silent, digital, and brutally effective.

Zara was the one who found it. She stormed into the bakery, her usual vibrant energy replaced by a cold, white-hot fury. She didn't say a word just slammed her phone down on the counter where Holly and Noel were reviewing the Gala's musical program.

"You need to see this," she said tightly.

The article was on a popular regional lifestyle blog the kind read by tens of thousands across New England, and the kind the contest judges would almost certainly follow. The headline was a punch to the gut:

"A TALE OF TWO TOWNS: PINE RIDGE CELEBRATES AN AUTHENTIC CHRISTMAS WHILE RIVAL EVERGREEN HOLLOW HIRES A CORPORATE GHOST."

Holly felt the blood drain from her face as she read. It was a masterpiece of subtle character assassination. The first half was a glowing tribute to Pine Ridge, lauding their "heartfelt, homespun" efforts. It described their plans for a *Community Memory Wall* featuring historical photos and a "grand, traditional Tree Gala" with a community sing-along a blatant, almost word-for-word theft of Holly's own ideas.

But the second half of the article was the real poison. It pivoted to Evergreen Hollow, framing their renaissance not as a community effort but as a cynical, corporate campaign. It mentioned Noel by name:

"...a high-priced architectural designer from Chicago, Noel Bishop, whose firm is best known for creating sleek, multi-million-dollar commercial installations for luxury brands like Valmont and Acheron."

It implied that Evergreen Hollow, unable to win on its own merits, had sold its soul hiring an outsider to manufacture a festive feeling.

The worst part, the one that made Holly's stomach clench with nausea, was the photo. It was a grainy, unflattering shot clearly taken with a long lens of the monstrous yellow crane from the day of the blackout, looming over the town square. The caption read:

Evergreen Hollow's idea of "community spirit"? Bringing in heavy industrial equipment, a move which residents say resulted in a town-wide power outage.

"They're twisting everything," Holly whispered, her hands trembling. "They're taking our story and using it as a weapon against us."

Noel read the article over her shoulder, his expression growing colder with every word. This wasn't just small-town rivalry; it was a professional hit job. He recognized the tactics the carefully chosen quotes, the out-of-context photo, the strategic framing of him as a corporate villain. It was designed to undermine his credibility, yes but more than that, it was designed to invalidate Holly's heart, to paint her authentic efforts as a manufactured lie. It was an attack on both of them, hitting them right on the fault line of their original conflict.

News of the article spread through town like wildfire. The hopeful energy of the morning evaporated, replaced by a grim, paranoid gloom. The happy buzz in the bakery died down to hushed, angry whispers. Volunteers who had been eagerly signing up for Gala shifts were suddenly hesitant, their confidence shaken.

Frank Henderson appeared at the bakery door, not with his usual smugness but with weary resignation. "I saw the article," he said to Holly, his voice heavy. "This is what I was afraid of. You put a target on our backs, and now the whole region thinks we're a laughingstock a bunch of country bumpkins who had to hire a city slicker to teach us how to hang tinsel."

The words, though not entirely unkind, hit their mark. The fragile unity they had built was beginning to fracture under the pressure. All the old doubts and insecurities were resurfacing.

"We need to fix this," Holly said, her voice trembling with a mix of rage and heartbreak. She, Noel, and Zara huddled around the oak table in the back of the bakery, the offending article glowing on the phone between them like a toxic ember.

"I'm going to write a letter to the editor," she said. "I'm going to tell them the truth how Pine Ridge stole our ideas, how they took that photo out of context, how Noel grew up here, how "

"No," Noel interrupted quietly but firmly.

Holly and Zara both stopped and looked at him.

"What do you mean, no?" Zara demanded. "We have to fight back!"

"A public, emotional denial is exactly what they want," Noel said, slipping into his strategic mode. He was no longer just Holly's partner he was the professional who understood this kind of warfare. "It makes us look defensive and petty. It keeps their story in the news cycle. We'd be playing their game by their rules. We can't win a mud-slinging match. We have to change the game."

"How?" Holly asked, her anger giving way to grudging respect for his calm logic.

"We don't win by *telling* people we're authentic," he said, locking eyes with her. "We win by *showing* them in a way so undeniable it makes their article look like the cheap shot it is. We don't get angry. We get smarter."

He leaned forward, his energy shifting from defensive to offensive. "They attacked us on two fronts: they stole our ideas, and they framed me as the corporate villain. So, we lean into what they can't steal or copy. We accelerate the Memory Lane Project. Get Arthur Vance to finish every single frame and get them up this week. Let people see our real history held in frames built by a man who's refused to participate in this town for twenty years. You can't fake that kind of authenticity."

He continued, his voice gaining momentum. "And the Community Canvas we make it the centerpiece of the Gala. It's the one thing they absolutely cannot replicate. It's the physical embodiment of our town's heart."

Holly felt a flicker of her earlier fire return, fanned by the brilliance of his strategy. He wasn't dismissing her ideas he was weaponizing them.

"And what about the article?" she asked. "About the journalist who wrote it? We just let her get away with it?"

A slow, dangerous smile spread across Noel's face. "No. We don't let her get away with it. We invite her to the Evergreen Gala."

Zara and Holly stared at him, dumbfounded.

"Are you insane?" Zara said. "That's like inviting a wolf to your sheep-shearing festival."

"Exactly," Noel replied. "It's the boldest, most confident move we can make. We don't send an angry letter we send her a beautiful, simple invitation. *Dear Ms. Albright, We were so interested to read your take on our town's efforts. The story is so much more complex and beautiful than you can imagine. Please, be our guest of honour at the Evergreen Gala and see for yourself.*"

"It's a power move," he continued. "It says we have nothing to hide. It turns the other cheek, but it also throws down a gauntlet. If she's a real journalist, she'll have to come. And when she does we'll show her the truth."

It was terrifying, brilliant, and utterly perfect the ideal fusion of Holly's faith in the town's heart and Noel's strategic mind. It was bones and magic, weaponized.

That evening, a twenty-foot blank canvas was stretched across the side of Henderson's Hardware. It was a stark, daunting, and very public statement. The whole town seemed to be watching, their mood uncertain, waiting to see what would happen next. They had been hit hard, and this strange, silent canvas was their only response.

Noel walked with Holly to the base of the wall, carrying two large buckets of paint one evergreen, one cranberry red. He set them down and looked at her, his face serious in the twilight.

"They meant for that article to drive a wedge between us," he said quietly. "To make the town doubt you and to make you doubt me. To turn us back into what we were when I first got here."

"I know," she said softly.

"Are we going to let them?" he asked, his eyes searching hers.

She looked from the vast, empty canvas a symbol of their immense, terrifying task to his face. She saw no trace of the corporate consultant, no hint of the stranger who had once torn her plans apart. She saw her partner his eyes full of calm, unwavering confidence in her, in their town, in them.

"Not a chance," she said, her resolve hardening into steel.

He smiled and handed her a paintbrush. The attack from Pine Ridge had been designed to expose their weaknesses and tear them apart. But as Holly dipped the brush into the rich red paint, she knew it had failed. It had only burned away their remaining doubts, sharpened their purpose, and given them a common enemy.

Pine Ridge had started a fight but Holly and Noel were about to finish it. And they were going to do it with a masterpiece painted in the colors of home.

Chapter 16

The Weight of A Promise

The *Pine Ridge* article, intended as a poison dart, had produced an entirely unexpected side effect. It stripped away the last of Holly and Noel's pretenses. The attack had forced them to defend not just a project, but the very essence of their partnership and in doing so, had fused them together. The awkwardness that lingered after their kiss was replaced by a quiet, unshakable intimacy. They were a unit now, a *we* standing against an external threat, and that shared purpose became a balm for their complicated history.

This deeper connection was most palpable in the quiet hours after the town had gone to sleep. They had taken to working late on the Community Canvas, now their main focus. The massive, twenty-foot mural stretched across the side of Henderson's Hardware had become their shared space a world of their own beneath the cold, silent watch of the streetlights.

That night, a gentle snow was falling, the flakes hissing softly as they landed on the pavement. The only other sound was the rhythmic swish of their paintbrushes. They were laying down the foundational layer of the mural a deep twilight blue that represented the winter sky. They worked in easy silence, their movements synchronized, one beginning a brushstroke where the other left off, their colors blending seamlessly in the middle. The shared act of creating something beautiful from a blank wall felt profoundly intimate a metaphor for what was quietly unfolding between them.

The *Pine Ridge* article had been vicious, but it had also been a gift. It had forced Holly to see Noel not as the corporate ghost she'd once imagined, but as a fierce defender of her vision. And it had forced Noel to face the past he had spent a decade trying to outrun.

Feeling the strength of this new, unspoken trust, Holly finally found the courage to ask the question that had been humming beneath every conversation since his return. She paused in her painting, turned to him, and spoke with gentle curiosity rather than accusation.

"Noel," she began softly, her voice breaking the quiet night. "That article… it was so unfair. It made you sound like a stranger, like you were never one of us." She hesitated, the question she'd held for ten years finally surfacing. "Why did you stay away for so long? After you left for college, it felt like you just vanished. What happened?"

The question landed gently in the snowy silence, yet it carried the weight of a decade. Noel stopped painting. He stared at the half-finished canvas, at the infinite, empty space still waiting to be filled. He exhaled slowly, the mist of his breath curling in the cold air. He knew he couldn't deflect or hide behind excuses. She had offered him her trust, and she deserved the truth the whole truth.

"Come on," he said, his voice rough. "Let's go inside. It's a long story."

He led her not to his sterile office or the bakery's main room, but to the small table by the window where they had first truly collaborated. The scent of her world of buttercream and bread wrapped around them as she made two steaming mugs of tea. He waited until she sat down, until the warmth of the mug seeped into his hands, before he began.

"I was terrified," he said at last, the admission so simple and raw it startled them both. "From the moment I set foot on that university campus, I was completely, utterly terrified. I was a small-town kid on a scholarship, Holly. Everyone else was different the sons and daughters of famous architects and real estate moguls. They talked about summering in the Hamptons and skiing in Aspen. I'd spent my summer roofing with my dad."

He stared down into his mug, eyes lost in a past she'd never seen. "I felt like an imposter. A fraud. And our dream the Evergreen Project, the things we sketched on napkins right here in this bakery it suddenly seemed so small, so naïve. I was surrounded by brutalist architecture and post-modern theory, and I thought if I even mentioned our dream of a holly-leaf pavilion, they'd laugh me out of the room."

"So, I put my head down and worked," he continued, his voice low and steady. "I worked twice as hard as everyone else just to feel like I was keeping up. I was running on coffee and fear. The promise I made to you on the bridge that I would come back was the only thing that felt real. It was my North Star. Every all-nighter, every perfect grade, every step forward was for that to come back here as a success and lay the world at your feet so we could finally build it."

He fell silent, the weight of memory thick in the air. "And then I got the internship," he said quietly. "That phone call our last one. I was desperate for validation. When I got the offer, it was the first time I felt like I belonged, like I wasn't just some kid from Vermont playing dress-up. I was so high on the success, so caught up in the relief, that I couldn't hear what was in your voice. I mistook your silence for anger, for not understanding. I didn't hear the hurt. I didn't hear the fear. I was a selfish idiot, and I handled it so, so badly."

"The internship led to a job offer," he went on, the words tumbling out now like a confession long overdue. "And I got swept up. The projects got bigger, the budgets larger, the praise louder. And with every success, our dream our promise grew heavier. Every step forward for me in Chicago was a step further away from you, from Evergreen Hollow. The promise started to feel less like a North Star and more like an anchor. It reminded me of everything I was failing the life I was supposed to be building."

This, Holly realized, was the heart of it the part she had never truly considered.

"So, I stopped calling as much," he whispered. "Because every time I heard your voice, it reminded me of that weight. And then I stopped calling altogether. It was easier to bury myself in work, to chase the next promotion, the next award. I kept telling myself, *just one more success, just one more step, and then I'll be worthy then I'll come back.* But the goalposts kept moving. And then… too much time had passed. The silence got too big to break."

He finally met her eyes, and she saw the raw vulnerability there the fear he had been hiding for ten long years. "I was afraid to come back," he confessed, his voice cracking. "Afraid I still wasn't successful enough. And later, afraid that the man I'd become the corporate architect, the guy designing chrome reindeer wasn't the boy you'd loved. I was afraid you wouldn't recognize me. Or worse, that you would, and you'd be disappointed. It was easier to be a ghost, Holly. Easier to disappear than to face that."

Tears streamed down Holly's cheeks. All the anger she had clung to for a decade dissolved into a wave of aching empathy.

He hadn't left out of arrogance or indifference he had left out of love, and stayed away out of fear.

"Oh, Noel," she whispered, reaching across the table to cover his trembling hand. "You got it so wrong. We both did."

He looked up, confused, his eyes full of sorrow.

"While you were in Chicago, terrified of being a disappointment," she said, her voice thick with emotion, "I was here, terrified of being a burden."

She took a shaky breath and shared the secret she had kept for a decade the missing piece of their broken story. "Right around the time you got your internship, when you were so excited about your future, my grandmother got sick. Her first real diagnosis. The doctors didn't know what it was, only that it was bad. She was so scared, Noel. This bakery was her whole world, and she was terrified of losing it."

She squeezed his hand, forcing him to see the truth in her eyes. "My parents were already in Florida. I was all she had. I couldn't leave her. And I couldn't tell you. You were finally flying so full of hope and promise. The last thing I wanted was for you to feel obligated to come back, to let my problems become your anchor. I thought I was protecting you. I thought I was protecting our dream by letting you chase it, unburdened. So I let you believe I was angry for you leaving. I let you believe I was the one pushing you away."

The confession settled between them, heavy and heartbreaking. It hadn't been a single misunderstanding it was two monumental sacrifices, two hearts breaking under the weight of unspoken, protective love. The ghosts that had haunted them for ten years weren't born of anger or abandonment; they were born of good intentions, of love so deep they destroyed it trying to save it.

The last of the ice didn't just crack it shattered into a thousand pieces, swept away by a flood of truth. He looked at her with dawning, horrified understanding; she looked back with forgiveness he never believed he deserved.

They didn't speak for a long time. There were no words for the immensity of what they had lost to silence and fear.

Finally, they stepped out into the cold pre-dawn air. The snow had stopped, and the eastern sky had softened to a promising gray. They stood before the Community Canvas, which no longer looked like an empty wall, but a symbol a place to paint a new beginning.

Noel picked up a brush, his movements slow and deliberate, and handed it to her. His eyes were clear for the first time, free of the shadows of his past.

"No more ghosts," he said, his voice thick but steady. "Just us."

Holly took the brush, her fingers steady around it. The weight of the old promise the one he had carried like a stone for ten years was gone. In its place was the fragile, luminous lightness of a new promise, one made without words but with understanding.

The path was finally clear.

Chapter 17

A Box of Old Sketches

The morning after their shared confessions felt like the first day of a new season. The air in Evergreen Hollow was still cold, but the biting, oppressive chill had been replaced by a clean, crisp brightness. Inside The Rolling Pin, the change was even more profound. The ghosts had been laid to rest. The heavy, unspoken history that had shadowed every interaction between Holly and Noel was gone, replaced by the quiet, steady foundation of a truth finally told.

When Noel walked in, the awkwardness of the previous mornings had vanished. He carried two coffees from the diner at the end of the street one black for him, one with a cinnamon stick for her. He had remembered how she liked it. It was a small gesture, but it spoke volumes. It said, *I see you. I'm paying attention.*

"I figured your machine deserved a break," he said, placing the cup on the counter beside her as she kneaded a batch of her grandmother's famous cinnamon roll dough.

"My hero," she said with an easy, genuine smile. "You have no idea how tired I am of the smell of my own coffee."

They stood in a comfortable, domestic silence for a moment, the rhythm of the bakery a familiar backdrop to their new peace. The frantic, desperate energy that had fueled the project was gone. In its place was a calm, focused determination. The contest, the threat from Pine Ridge, the weight of the town's expectations it was all still there, but it no longer felt like a battle to be survived. It felt like a project to be enjoyed.

"I was thinking last night," Holly said, sprinkling a generous layer of cinnamon and sugar over a sheet of rolled-out dough. "About the Gala. The skating rink needs a warming hut. A real one not just a tent. A place where people can get out of the wind and drink their hot chocolate."

"Good idea," Noel said, his mind immediately clicking into gear. "Structurally simple. We could get the high school woodshop to frame it. We'd need a design, a blueprint…"

Holly paused, her expression softening with nostalgia. "You know… I think we already have one. We drew it years ago a little log cabin design with a big stone fireplace. Where did we put all that old stuff? That box…"

A shared look of understanding passed between them the *Evergreen Project* box. The time capsule she had opened alone in a moment of despair was now something they could unearth together, in a moment of hope.

"The attic," she said, her eyes lighting up with the thrill of the hunt. "I think my grandmother stored it above the bakery."

The attic was a forgotten world, bathed in soft, dusty light filtering through a single, grimy porthole window. It smelled of cedar wood, old paper, and a century of captured time. It was a library of her family's history her grandfather's army trunk, stacks of her mother's yearbooks, and her grandmother's collection of antique baking tins.

They moved through the space together, their footsteps stirring up clouds of dancing dust motes. It was Noel who found it tucked away under a heavy canvas tarp. A simple, sturdy cardboard box, its edges softened with age. On the top, in youthful, looping cursive unmistakably Holly's, were the words: **THE EVERGREEN PROJECT.**

They carried it down from the attic as if it were a sacred artifact, placing it in a patch of sunlight on the great oak table in the bakery. For a moment, they just stared at it this tangible piece of their shared soul.

"Ready?" he asked softly.

She nodded.

He lifted the lid. The scent that rose to meet them was the smell of their own past: old paper, pencil graphite, and the faint, sweet trace of a chocolate bar one of them had probably smuggled into a late-night planning session.

Slowly, reverently, they began to pull out the sketches. Each one was a portal to a specific memory, a specific dream. The first few were fantastical, impossible ones and they laughed.

"The gingerbread clocktower," Noel said, holding up a detailed drawing of a magnificent structure with licorice hands and gumdrop numbers. "I was so proud of this. I remember calculating the structural integrity of the gingerbread as if that were a real thing."

"I was the one who insisted on the marshmallow-fluff snow on the roof," Holly admitted, her cheeks pink with laughter. "You told me the moisture content would compromise the whole building."

"Spoken like a true architect," he said, his eyes twinkling. It was the first time they had been able to laugh at their past to see its youthful naïveté not as a source of pain, but as something precious and pure.

They found other, more practical ideas: detailed plans for the hand-painted wooden signs they had wanted to place around town, and a unique starburst pattern for stringing lights on the main Christmas tree a design so good they both agreed, in a moment of shared excitement, that they had to use it this year.

Then Noel pulled out a sheet of paper that made him fall silent. It wasn't a blueprint. It was a series of stunningly detailed charcoal portraits of familiar townspeople a laughing Mrs. Gable, a thoughtful Mr. Blackwood, a grumpy but secretly soft Silas Hemlock each face capturing a perfect, candid moment of emotion.

"Holly," he breathed, his voice full of rediscovered awe. "I forgot how good you were at this. Not just the buildings the people." He looked up at her, his expression serious. "This is what I was missing in my own work. I can design a beautiful room, but you… you know how to fill it with life. You see the faces. The heart."

A moment later, Holly found a sketch that was pure Noel a technically brilliant cross-section of a heated bench for the skating rink, showing the intricate network of pipes and heating elements that would circulate warm water through the seat. It was a design born not just of cleverness, but of a deep, innate empathy.

"I remember this," she said softly. "You spent a week on it. You were so determined to make sure no one's parents got cold while they were watching their kids skate." She looked at him, a new understanding dawning in her eyes. "You were always trying to make things better, not just prettier. You were always trying to take care of people, even then."

He had cared for them with engineering and physics; she had cared for them with art and emotion. It was the same impulse, expressed in two different languages.

And then, at the very bottom of the box, they found it the master sketch. The elegant rendering of the holly-leaf pavilion, their names written in the corner: *Sutton & Bishop, Lead Architects.*

They looked at it together, and this time, there was no pain, no bitterness. The memory was not a ghost of what they had lost but a beacon of what they had found again. The dream wasn't dead it had only been dormant, waiting for them to be ready.

A new, powerful creative energy sparked between them. This wasn't just about reminiscence anymore; it was about resurrection.

"The warming hut," Noel said, excitement buzzing in his voice. He grabbed his tablet. "Let's build it. Your design."

Holly picked up a fresh sheet of parchment and a charcoal pencil. "Only if we build your heated benches to go with it."

What followed was a beautiful, seamless blur of creation. They were no longer two people trying to compromise they were one mind, a perfect fusion of art and architecture. He took her whimsical, two-dimensional sketch of the log-cabin warming hut and, with a few taps on his tablet, rendered it as a stunning three-dimensional model. He showed her how they could use reclaimed timber from the old mill to give it authentic history, how a few simple structural tweaks could make it both sturdy and elegant.

She, in turn, took his brilliant but purely functional design for the heated bench and gave it magic. She sketched a new, more organic shape a gentle, curving form that echoed the rolling hills surrounding the town. She added intricate carved details into the backrest patterns of holly leaves and snowflakes that transformed it from an engineering project into a work of art.

They worked in a flurry of excited, overlapping sentences, their creative shorthand a language only they understood.

"If we angle the roofline just so," he said, adjusting the 3D model, "the morning sun will hit the fireplace."

"And we can put a window right here," she added, sketching furiously, "so you can see the big tree from inside while you're warming up."

They were rebuilding their dream not as it had been, but as it was now: stronger, wiser, tempered by time and truth. It was the ultimate fulfillment of the promise they had made on the bridge all those years ago a promise to build things that mattered, together.

As the afternoon sun dipped low, casting long golden stripes of light through the bakery windows, they leaned back, surrounded by a happy, chaotic mess of old sketches and new blueprints. The bakery was quiet; the last of the customers had long gone.

Noel gently picked up the old drawing of the holly-leaf pavilion, his expression thoughtful and serene.

"You know," he said quietly, his tone calm but certain, "after this is all over... I think we could actually build this. For real."

It was a new promise but this one was different. It wasn't the grand, desperate vow of an eighteen-year-old boy trying to prove his worth. It was a quiet statement of intent from a man who had finally found his way home. It was not a weight; it was a foundation.

Holly looked at him, at the sincerity in his eyes, and a deep, peaceful smile spread across her face. She didn't need to say anything. He was right. They could. And they would.

Later, as they cleaned up their creative explosion, they carefully placed the old sketches back in the time-capsule box. They weren't burying the past anymore; they were protecting it honoring it. They put the box on a high shelf in Holly's office, a place of respect.

Then they took their new, combined designs the beautiful, practical warming hut and the elegant, empathetic heated bench and pinned them side by side on the main planning board in the center of the bakery. The old dreams had become new reality, the past and present finally, perfectly aligned. The tangled memories had been straightened and woven into a future stronger and more beautiful than anything they had ever imagined.

Chapter 18

What We Left Unsaid

In the wake of their creative breakthrough, a new rhythm settled over their days. The frantic, crisis-driven pace of the project's beginning had been replaced by a steady, productive hum. The town, now a well-oiled machine of community spirit, was running on its own momentum. The various committees Holly had established were taking ownership of their tasks with newfound pride. Arthur Vance was delivering his beautiful, handcrafted frames ahead of schedule. Zara had organized the volunteer roster for the Evergreen Gala with the precision of a military general. For the first time, Holly and Noel found themselves with something they hadn't had since his arrival: moments of quiet.

These pockets of peace were unfamiliar territory. Their relationship had been forged and reforged in the heat of conflict, collaboration, and crisis. Now, in the calm, they were left with the simple, terrifying, and wonderful reality of just being two people in a room together.

The routine they'd fallen into was a comfortable one. Noel would finish his work at his sterile temporary office and then migrate to The Rolling Pin in the late afternoon, just as Holly was starting to clean up. He'd help her wipe down tables or sweep the floor these simple, domestic acts were quiet statements of his intention to be a part of her world, not just a visitor in it.

Tonight, the bakery was especially peaceful. A heavy, silent snow was falling outside, blanketing Main Street in a thick layer of white and muffling the world into serene stillness. The last customer had departed, and Holly was slowly wiping down the gleaming espresso machine, the rhythmic motion a soothing end to a long day. Noel was sweeping, his movements easy and practiced, his presence a comforting weight in the warm, fragrant space. The air was thick with the scent of yeast and melting butter, and the only sounds were the swish of his broom and the gentle ticking of the clock.

In this profound quiet, with the ghosts of their past finally laid to rest, Holly found herself curious about a different set of specters: the lives they had lived apart. She knew the broad strokes of his story the fear and ambition that had driven him but she didn't know the details. She didn't know the man who had lived and breathed during that decade-long gap.

She finished cleaning and leaned against the counter.

"You know," she began softly, breaking the comfortable silence, "you told me all about the pressure and fear of your job, but you never really told me if you were ever… happy. In Chicago." She paused, then asked the question that felt both impossibly bold and absolutely necessary. "Was there ever anyone? A serious anyone?"

Noel stopped sweeping. He leaned the broom against the wall, the simple act feeling deliberate, significant. He looked at her, his expression open and unguarded in the soft light of the bakery. He didn't deflect or hesitate. He knew this conversation was as important as the one about their breakup it was about the ten years they had to reclaim.

"Yeah," he said, his voice a low, honest rumble. "There was. One."

He walked over to their now-customary table by the window and sat down. Holly poured the last of the day's coffee into two mugs and joined him.

"Her name was Amelia," he began, staring down into his cup. "We met at the firm. She was a project manager smart, ambitious, beautiful. We were a perfect match on paper. We dated for almost two years."

Holly felt a small, irrational pang of something she refused to name. She just nodded, listening.

"She was great," he continued, his tone sincere. "We had fun. We traveled. We went to gallery openings and talked about brutalist architecture. We looked like the perfect, successful couple." He let out a short, mirthless laugh. "But it was all… surface level. With me, anyway. I could never fully let her in. I was there, but I wasn't. It was like I was holding a part of myself in reserve."

He finally looked up, his eyes locking with hers, full of a dawning, painful understanding.

"She's the one who ended it. I'll never forget what she said. We were in our beautiful, minimalist apartment that never felt like home, and she just looked at me and said, 'It feels like I'm dating a ghost, Noel. Like you're saving the best part of yourself the real part for someone else.' I didn't understand it then. I thought she was being dramatic." He shook his head, regret flickering in his eyes. "I didn't realize until I came back here until I was standing in this bakery again that she was right. I was saving it for you."

The confession hung between them a stunning, heartfelt admission. He had been emotionally faithful to her memory, even when he hadn't realized it.

"What about you?" he asked gently. "Ten years is a long time. There must have been someone."

Holly thought of the few men she had dated over the years. Good men. Kind men. Men who were not Noel.

"There was one who was… almost serious," she admitted, tracing the rim of her coffee mug. "His name was Ben. He was the town vet. Kind, funny, and he loved this town as much as I do. Everyone adored him. My grandmother adored him." She smiled a small, sad smile. "It was perfect, on paper."

She echoed his words without realizing it, and they both acknowledged it with a shared, knowing look.

"We dated for about a year," she said. "It was nice. Comfortable. He was safe. But that's all it ever was. It never felt like fire it felt like a warm blanket. And one day, I realized I was suffocating." She looked out the window at the falling snow. "He was a wonderful man, but it never felt like coming home. I was always comparing him to a ghost to a boy who understood that I wanted to build fantastical buildings, not just bake bread. No matter how kind Ben was, he could never compete with the memory of you."

She finally admitted the truth she had barely allowed herself to acknowledge.

"I was so busy taking care of everyone else's memories," she whispered, her gaze drifting to the photo of her grandmother, "that I didn't think I was allowed to make any new ones for myself. So, I stayed with the ghosts. It was safer."

They sat in silence, their stories laid bare on the old oak table. They weren't just the teenagers who had fallen in love on a bridge anymore. They were two adults who had tried and failed to build lives without each other, haunted by a past they had never fully understood.

He, the lonely ghost of his own success.

She, the lonely curator of a town's memories.

In sharing the stories of the people they had been, they finally, truly saw the people they had become. She saw past the corporate architect to the lonely, driven man who had lost his way. He saw past the small-town baker to the strong, resilient woman who had carried the weight of a town on her shoulders. They weren't falling in love with a memory anymore they were falling in love with the complex, flawed, beautiful adults sitting across from each other in the quiet of a snow-filled night.

The conversation wound down, leaving a deep, peaceful stillness in its wake. There were no more secrets. Nothing left unsaid.

Noel reached across the table, his hand covering hers. His touch was warm, steady, and sure.

"No more ghosts, Holly," he said, his voice a low, solemn promise.

He stood, gently pulling her to her feet. He didn't say anything else. He didn't need to. He framed her face with his hands, his gaze searching hers, asking a silent question. She answered by leaning into him, her hands resting on his chest, feeling the steady beat of his heart beneath her palms.

The kiss, when it came, was nothing like the one on the bridge. That one had been a question a shock, a rekindling. This was an answer. A deliberate, conscious choice made by two people who saw each other completely, flaws and all, and chose each other anyway.

It was a kiss of profound intimacy deeper and more certain than any they had shared before. It was passionate, yes, but it was also filled with deep, soulful tenderness. It wasn't about what was lost; it was about the infinite, beautiful possibility of what they were finally finding. It was a kiss that closed a ten-year-old chapter and began a brand-new one.

When they finally broke apart, they didn't speak. They just held each other a long, quiet embrace in the middle of the dark, fragrant bakery. His arms were strong and sure around her, and for the first time in a very long time, Holly felt the exhausting weight of being the sole keeper of the flame begin to lift. She wasn't alone anymore. She was home.

Later, they walked out of the bakery hand in hand into the silent, sleeping town. The fresh snow crunched under their boots the only sound in the pristine world. In the distance, the lights they had hung on the Old Town Bridge cast a steady golden glow, a beacon in the winter night. They were no longer walking a tightrope between the past and the present. For the first time, they were walking together, on solid ground, into the hopeful, glittering light of a shared future.

Chapter 19

The Midpoint on The Bridge

The days that followed their final confession felt like waking from a long, troubled dream. The world once shadowed by unspoken history and regret was now sharp, clear, and full of a light that seemed to shine from the simple, profound fact of their togetherness. The ghosts had not only been laid to rest; they had been lovingly packed away, honored for the lessons they had taught, and replaced by the vibrant, living presence of the here and now.

Their relationship, now an open and happy secret, had become the town's silent, beating heart. There was no grand announcement only a series of small, telling moments that Evergreen Hollow, with its expert knowledge of its own, observed with quiet, collective satisfaction. It was Noel showing up at the bakery before it opened with coffee, just for her. It was Holly resting her head on his shoulder for a brief, weary moment during a late-night planning session. It was the easy, unconscious way they now reached for each other's hand as they walked down Main Street. The town saw it, and the town approved. The project, once a desperate battle for survival, had transformed into a joyful act of creation a town-wide celebration of a love story a decade in the making.

With the Evergreen Gala just one week away, the project had reached its midpoint. The initial chaos of planning had given way to the focused hum of execution. Arthur Vance's beautiful frames now lined the path to the Town Hall, each one a glowing tribute to the past. The Community Canvas was a riot of color a beautiful, chaotic masterpiece of handprints, hopeful words, and crudely drawn but heartfelt pictures of homes and trees. The entire town was a beehive of purposeful activity, and at its center were Holly and Noel.

On a crisp, clear late afternoon, with the sun casting long, blue shadows across the snow, Noel found Holly in the bakery, staring at the master planning board, a worried little frown on her face.

"What's wrong?" he asked, his voice a low, comforting rumble as he came to stand behind her, his hands resting gently on her shoulders.

"Nothing's wrong," she sighed, leaning back into his touch. "Everything is… right. Too right. I'm just waiting for the other shoe to drop."

He smiled, pressing a light kiss to the top of her head. "No more dropped shoes. We've got this." He took her hand, his fingers lacing through hers. "Come on. Let's take a break a real one. For an hour. We've earned it."

He didn't have to say where they were going. There was only one place.

They walked to the Old Town Bridge in comfortable silence, their boots crunching in the snow. The bridge was no longer a place of ghosts or near-misses; it was their sanctuary. The warm, golden lights they had hung together flickered on as the twilight deepened, casting a magical, welcoming glow.

They stopped in the middle at their window leaning against the railing where their initials were carved, a permanent mark of their story's beginning and its new chapter. The river below was a dark, quiet ribbon, the world hushed and peaceful.

"Can you believe it?" Holly said, her voice full of soft wonder as she looked at the glowing lights. "A few weeks ago, we were standing in this exact spot, practically strangers, fighting about everything."

"I wasn't a stranger," he corrected her gently. "I was just… lost, and trying to pretend I wasn't." He looked down at their intertwined hands, then back at her face, his expression full of deep, settled love. "You brought me home, Holly. Not just to Evergreen Hollow home to myself."

"And you," she said, her voice thick with emotion, "you reminded me that it's okay to dream of a future, not just protect the past. You took my blueprints the ones I had hidden away and told me we could still build them."

This was the true midpoint a moment of quiet reflection on the journey they had taken together. It wasn't just about the contest anymore. It was about the two of them, standing on the foundation of their healed past, looking toward a future that was, for the first time, a shared horizon.

"What happens after?" she asked softly, her question small but significant. "After the contest, after the judging, after the winner is announced… what happens then?"

It was the question they had both been avoiding the one that hovered at the edge of their newfound happiness. His life, his career, his entire world was in Chicago. Hers was here, rooted as deeply as the old pines on the mountainside.

Noel turned to her, his expression serious. He took both of her hands in his. "I don't have all the answers yet, Hol. But I know one thing. My life in Chicago it's just a collection of stuff in an apartment I was never really in. It's a job that paid the bills but left me empty. It's not a home. This," he said, his gaze sweeping over the glowing town, then landing, with profound intensity, back on her face, "this is home. You are home. And I am done running away from it."

He continued, his voice steady with calm, unwavering certainty. "I don't know what it'll look like. Maybe I open a small design studio here. Maybe we find a way to split our time. Maybe we just take it one day at a time. But I'm not leaving you again. That's one promise I'll spend the rest of my life keeping."

Tears of pure joy welled in Holly's eyes. It was everything she had ever hoped to hear everything the sixteen-year-old girl who had carved her initials into this bridge had ever dreamed of.

Just as she was about to reply, the sound of slow, heavy footsteps echoed on the bridge's wooden planks. They turned to see Frank Henderson walking toward them. His usual disapproving frown was gone, replaced by a look of weary, grudging respect.

He stopped a few feet away, his gaze on the glowing Memory Lane frames. "Arthur Vance is doing good work," he said the words sounding like a major concession coming from him. He looked at the two of them, standing there hand in hand. "The town feels... different. Better." He cleared his throat, looking almost embarrassed. "My father would have liked all this the old pictures. He would have liked seeing the town remember." He gave them a curt, almost imperceptible nod, then continued on his way, leaving a stunned silence in his wake.

"Did Frank Henderson just give us his blessing?" Holly whispered in amazement.

"I think he did," Noel said, a slow grin spreading across his face. "Now I know we're going to win."

They laughed a shared, happy sound that filled the quiet air of the bridge. As their laughter faded, Noel's phone buzzed in his pocket. He pulled it out, his smile dimming slightly as he looked at the screen.

It was a text from his boss in Chicago: *Project in London just moved up. HUGE. Need you back ASAP for the pitch. This is the one we've been waiting for.*

Holly saw the change in his expression the slight dimming of the light in his eyes. "What is it?" she asked.

He looked from the phone, that small, glowing portal to the big, shiny world he had left behind, to her face, her beautiful, beloved face full of trust and hope. He made a choice. He silenced the phone, the screen going dark, and slipped it back into his pocket, dismissing it completely.

"It's nothing," he said, his smile returning, his focus entirely on her. "Just work spam. It can wait."

He pulled her closer, his arms wrapping around her waist. "Now, where were we?" he murmured, his lips finding hers in a kiss that was deep, sweet, and full of the promise of a future that felt as solid and enduring as the old bridge beneath their feet.

They left the bridge a little while later, hand in hand, ready to face the final, frantic week of preparations. They were stronger than ever their love a beacon as bright as the lights they had hung together. But as they walked away, the silenced phone in Noel's pocket felt like a small, quiet ticking clock a reminder that the outside world, with its own grand plans and glittering promises, had not forgotten him, even if he, for this perfect, fleeting moment, had forgotten it.

Chapter 20

A Lost Letter

A profound and settled peace had become the new normal for Holly and Noel. In the final, frantic week leading up to the Evergreen Gala, their partnership was the calm, steady eye of the hurricane. The town buzzed with joyful, purposeful energy around them, but they moved through it all with a quiet intimacy that felt sacred. They were a self-contained universe of two their shared past no longer a source of pain, but a rich, foundational soil from which something new and beautiful was growing.

This newfound domesticity was most evident in the evenings. After the last volunteer had gone home and the final planning detail for the day had been checked off, Noel would walk Holly up to her small, cozy apartment above the bakery. It was a space entirely her own, filled with stacks of books, colorful woven blankets, and the faint, lingering scent of vanilla and old paper. For Noel, who had spent a decade in vast, minimalist spaces that echoed with emptiness, Holly's apartment felt like the warmest, safest place on earth.

Tonight, they were engaged in a simple domestic task: clearing out an old storage closet to make room for the boxes of custom-printed programs for the Gala. Holly had pulled out a large cardboard box of her grandmother's old things, her laughter soft as she sorted through the contents.

"Look at this," she said, holding up a recipe card for a "Jell-O and Marshmallow Delight," the instructions written in her grandmother's elegant cursive. "A true culinary horror from 1972. I think she made this for my dad's tenth birthday."

"My mom had the same recipe," Noel chuckled, sorting through a stack of old, sepia-toned photographs. "I think it was a mandatory dish for that entire generation."

They worked in easy harmony, sharing stories, their shoulders brushing as they reached into the box. It was in these small, unglamorous moments that their future felt most real most tangible. This was what a life together could be: not grand gestures or dramatic reunions, but the simple, profound comfort of being in the same room, sharing the same small patch of quiet.

Holly reached the bottom of the box, her fingers brushing against a bundle of letters tied with a faded blue silk ribbon. "Oh, these are the letters from her sister in California," she said, smiling fondly. As she lifted the bundle out, a single, separate envelope that had been tucked underneath slid free and landed on the floor.

It was different from the others a standard business-sized envelope, slightly crumpled and gray with age. But the handwriting on the front made Holly's breath catch in her throat. It was sharp, architectural, and achingly familiar. It was Noel's. It was addressed simply to: **Holly Sutton, The Rolling Pin, Evergreen Hollow, VT.**

"Noel," she whispered, her voice suddenly tight.

He looked over, his smile fading as he saw what she was holding. He knelt beside her on the floor, his eyes fixed on the impossible object in her hand. The postmark was clear from his old college town in Massachusetts, dated November 12th, ten years ago just three days after their last, terrible phone call. But there was no stamp.

Tucked just under the unsealed flap, almost invisible, was a tiny, folded note. Holly's hands trembled as she opened it. The script was her grandmother's. It said:

"Found this in the pocket of your father's old winter coat. He must have forgotten all those years ago. So sorry, my dear."

A sudden, breathless silence filled the small apartment. The air grew thick with the presence of a ghost they hadn't even known existed. This was a missing piece a lost message from a past they thought they had completely understood.

Holly looked at Noel, her eyes wide with a silent question. He stared at the letter, his face pale, his mind clearly reeling back through a decade of pain to a moment of desperate, youthful heartbreak he had tried so hard to bury.

"I... I barely remember writing it," he said, his voice a hoarse whisper. "I just remember the feeling that I had broken the most important thing in my life and I had to fix it." He looked at her, his eyes full of raw, ancient pain. "You should read it."

With trembling fingers, Holly carefully opened the flap. The paper inside was thin the kind a desperate college student might use covered in dense, slightly frantic lines of ink. She unfolded it, took a deep, steadying breath, and began to read aloud.

"My Holly,

I'm so sorry. I'm so, so sorry for how our call went. I was an idiot. I was so caught up in my own news that I didn't listen, and I know I hurt you. Please, please forgive me.

This internship… it's not about leaving you. It's the opposite. It's the first real step toward building everything we ever talked about. These people, this firm they're the best in the world. If I can learn from them, I can learn how to actually build our Evergreen Project, not just dream about it. I'm doing this for us. I promise.

I know you feel like you're holding me back sometimes. I heard it in your voice. But you have to know, Holly that's the most wrong you could ever be. You're not holding me back; you're the only thing holding me together. This place… it's hard. I feel like I'm pretending all the time. The thought of you, of our bridge, of our future that's the only thing that's real. That's my North Star.

Please don't give up on us. I know I'm far away, but my heart is right there in Evergreen Hollow, in that bakery with you. I'll work this internship, I'll save every penny, and I'll come home for Christmas. And when I do, I'll have a real plan, a real blueprint, and we can finally start. Just please, please wait for me. Keep believing in us.

It's still you, Hol. It's always been you.

Please just call me. Tell me we're okay.

All my love, forever,

Noel"

The letter fell from Holly's fingers onto the floor. A strangled sob escaped her throat as a decade of carefully constructed narrative the story of a boy who had left and never looked back, who had chosen ambition over her was utterly demolished by the desperate, loving, hopeful words of the boy himself.

He hadn't abandoned her. He had been fighting for them. He had been just as scared and just as heartbroken as she was.

Noel watched her, his face a mask of anguish. He reached out and picked up the letter, his gaze falling on his own youthful, desperate plea. The memories flooded back the late night in the library, scribbling words through tears, pouring every ounce of his heart onto the page, the flicker of hope as he'd sealed it.

"Your dad," he said, the pieces finally clicking into place with horrifying clarity. "Your dad was visiting his cousin just outside Boston that weekend. I met him for coffee. I gave it to him. I asked him to give it to you in person. I thought... I thought it would mean more than just putting it in the mail."

"And he must have put it in his coat pocket," Holly whispered, finishing the tragic story. "And he just... forgot."

Her father had been famously absent-minded, his head always full of fishing lures and half-finished woodworking projects. It was such a simple, innocent, and devastatingly human mistake. There was no villain in their story. No grand betrayal. Only the quiet, heartbreaking cruelty of a single, forgotten letter.

"All this time," she choked out, the tears she'd held back for ten years finally falling freely, "I thought you didn't want me anymore. I thought your world had just gotten too big for me."

"And I thought you'd given up on me," he said, his voice thick with unshed tears as he knelt in front of her, taking her hands in his. "I waited for you to call. And when you didn't...

I thought your silence was the answer. I thought I had broken us beyond repair."

They were no longer defined by the misunderstanding but by the shared, tragic nobility of what they had tried to do. Two scared kids, trying to protect each other and their shared dream and in doing so, shattering it completely.

He gently pulled her into his arms, and she buried her face in his shoulder, her sobs shaking her body. He held her, stroking her hair, his own tears falling silently into it. It was an embrace that held a decade of pain, loneliness, and what-ifs. It was the final, absolute release of every ghost that had ever stood between them.

After the storm of tears passed, a deep, quiet peace settled in the room. They were curled up together on her small sofa, her head resting on his chest, his arms wrapped securely around her. The lost letter the artifact of their tragic history lay on the coffee table. It no longer looked like a symbol of pain. It looked like a key.

"I love you," she whispered into the soft fabric of his sweater. "I never stopped."

"I love you, too," he murmured into her hair, his voice thick with emotion. "I was just too afraid to come home and say it."

Just then, his phone, which he'd left on the end table, buzzed with an incoming text. The sound, which a few days ago would have felt like an intrusion, now seemed distant and unimportant. He glanced at it another message from his boss about the London project, this one more urgent.

He picked up the phone and, without hesitation, showed it to Holly. There were no more secrets between them.

She read the message, then looked up at him, her expression calm and unafraid.

"You'll have to deal with that eventually," she said softly.

"I know." He looked from the glowing screen a portal to a life of chrome reindeer and hollow victories to her face, the face of his entire world. He typed a quick reply: *My priorities are here right now. I'll be in touch when I can.* He sent it, then turned the phone off completely, tossing it onto the armchair across the room.

"But not tonight," he said, pulling her closer. "Tonight, there is nothing in the world but this."

The lost letter had answered the final, painful question of their past. Now, wrapped in each other's arms in the quiet, snow-covered town, there were no more questions at all only the peaceful, steady, unbreakable certainty of a love that had, against all odds, finally found its way home.

Chapter 21

The Reason I Stayed

The morning after the discovery of the lost letter dawned bright and impossibly clear. A fresh blanket of snow had fallen overnight, and the world outside Holly's apartment window was a pristine, glittering expanse of white. Inside, the atmosphere was one of profound peace. The final, ragged edges of their past had been smoothed over, leaving only the deep, steady certainty of their shared present.

They sat at Holly's small kitchen table, a place designed for one that now felt perfectly suited for two. Noel had insisted on making breakfast, moving around her kitchen with an easy, confident grace that was surprisingly domestic. The scent of sizzling bacon and fresh coffee filled the small space, mingling with the ever-present sweetness drifting up from the bakery below. It was the perfect blend of his world and hers.

As they ate, their conversation was light, easy, and full of the simple joy of rediscovery. He learned that she hated the crusts on her toast; she learned that he took his coffee with an appalling amount of sugar. They were filling in the small, intimate details of who they were now not just who they had been.

Noel paused, his fork hovering over his plate, his expression thoughtful and gentle.

"Last night… hearing my side of the story, it explained so much. But it's only half the picture."

He looked at her, his eyes full of deep, searching empathy.

"You said your grandmother was sick, Holly, but you never really talked about it. What was it like for you? After I left… after we stopped talking. I need to understand."

Holly looked down at her hands, wrapped around a warm mug. He deserved to know. Not the simple, shortened version she had given before, but the full, complicated truth. The story wasn't something she could easily tell with words alone it was written into the very fabric of the town.

"Walk with me," she said softly.

She led him not to the bridge or any of their romantic haunts, but on a different kind of tour a walk through the landscape of her own history. Their first stop was the heart of it all: the bakery.

They stood in the main room, the morning light streaming through the front window.

"It didn't happen all at once," she began, her voice low and steady. "Her illness was a slow fade, not a sudden fall. At first, it was small things. She'd forget a supplier's name. She'd put salt in the sugar bowl. We laughed about it, called it 'old-timer's disease.' I was going to the community college here, taking business classes, planning to transfer to a four-year school for design. I was just 'helping out' in the afternoons."

She led him into the small, cramped office in the back the place she had once hated, the place that had become the command center of her world.

"Then 'helping out' became handling the morning bake because she was too tired. Then it became managing the accounts because the numbers started confusing her. She'd get these terrible headaches, these moments of profound confusion where she wouldn't know where she was. And the only thing that calmed her down was the routine of this place the smell of the ovens, the feel of the dough."

Holly's gaze drifted to a worn, comfortable armchair tucked into the corner, an item that looked distinctly out of place in such a functional office.

"My drafting table used to be there," she said quietly. "The big, professional one my parents bought me for high school graduation. It took up half the room. One day, I came in and Grandma was just sitting on a hard, wooden stool, her head in her hands, looking so lost and frail. The next day, I sold the drafting table and bought her that chair, so she could sit comfortably and watch me work and still feel like she was part of things."

The tangible sacrifice the physical replacement of her dream with her duty hung in the air between them. Noel reached out and took her hand, his thumb brushing her knuckles, his silence more eloquent than any words.

Their next stop was the town library, a quiet, sunlit room that smelled of old books and lemon polish.

"This was my world for a few years," she said, gesturing to the small collection of architecture and design books in the corner. "My friends were all away at school, living these big, exciting lives. Zara would send me postcards from New York. Others were studying abroad in Europe. My life was the bakery, and home, and the twenty-foot walk between them. Every other Tuesday, when we had a home-care aide come in, I'd come here for two hours. It was my only escape. I'd read and sketch and try to remember the girl I used to be."

She pulled a heavy book from the shelf, its pages filled with photographs of modern architecture.

"I would look at these incredible buildings," she whispered, her voice thick with the memory of her loneliness, "and I'd feel this... ache. Like I was a ghost haunting the edges of a life someone else was living. I was happy for you, for the success I knew you were having. And I was so, so lonely."

But her story wasn't only one of sadness it was one of profound, bittersweet love. She led him to the small park behind the town hall, to a bench that overlooked the river.

"It wasn't all grim," she said with a soft smile. "In those last couple of years, when her memory of the present was almost gone, her memory of the past became incredibly vivid. We'd sit here, or in the bakery late at night, and she'd just... talk. She told me everything stories about her parents opening the bakery in the 1930s, about meeting my grandfather at a town dance. She told me the secret to her sourdough starter, which apparently goes back to the old country. She didn't just teach me how to run a business, Noel. She passed her whole life down to me. She made me the keeper of our family's story of this town's story."

She looked at him, her eyes shining with unshed tears.

"I thought my world had shrunk to the size of this town. But in those conversations, I realized my world was deeper than I'd ever imagined. I wasn't just taking care of her I was inheriting a legacy."

After her grandmother passed away, that legacy became her lifeline.

"I thought I would be alone," she confessed. "But the town... the town just wrapped its arms around me. Mrs. Gable brought me a casserole every night for a month. Silas Hemlock, who I was sure hated everyone, showed up one morning with his toolbox, fixed the leaky pipe under my sink, and refused to take a dime. They didn't see me as Eleanor Sutton's granddaughter anymore. They saw me as Holly the girl who stayed. The one who kept the heart of the town beating. I realized I hadn't just been taking care of my grandmother I'd been taking care of them too, in my own way. And they were taking care of me."

She had found a different kind of dream, she explained not one of steel and glass, but one of flour and community. A dream of belonging.

They ended their walk back on the Old Town Bridge, the place where all their stories, past and present, seemed to converge. The sun was high in the sky now, the day bright and full of life.

"You didn't get stuck here, Holly," Noel said, his voice full of quiet awe. He finally understood the whole picture the immense strength and love that had anchored her to this place. "You chose to stay. You chose to build something. Every single day."

A look of profound self-acceptance settled on Holly's face, the last of her ghosts finally laid to rest.

"For the longest time, I thought I'd given up my dream of being a designer," she said, her voice clear and strong. "But I realize now, I didn't. I was just designing something different. I was designing a community a safe place for people to land. It's not as grand as a skyscraper in Chicago, but it's built to last."

Noel reached into his coat pocket and pulled out the old, folded sketch of the holly-leaf pavilion. He had been carrying it with him, she realized, like a talisman. He gently unfolded it, the paper worn and soft with age.

"A good designer knows the most important part of any structure is the foundation," he said, his voice thick with emotion. He looked from the sketch to her face, his eyes full of love and admiration deeper and steadier than their teenage romance had ever been. "And you, Holly Sutton, have been building the foundation for this all along."

He leaned in and kissed her a deep, tender kiss full of respect. It honored not just the girl he had loved, but the incredible woman she had become.

When they broke apart, they stood in a comfortable, complete silence. The last of the unspoken had finally been said. The last of the *what-ifs* had been answered.

They were not two broken halves who had found each other. They were two whole, strong people who, after a decade of designing lives apart, had finally, truly chosen to design a future together.

They turned toward the town square, where the joyful preparations for the Gala were in full swing their shared past a solid bridge beneath their feet, leading them into the light of a shared future.

Chapter 22

The Reason I Left

The profound intimacy of Holly's story settled around them, forming a quiet, sacred space in the heart of the sleeping town. Noel had listened to every word, his heart aching with a mixture of love, admiration, and deep, sorrowful regret for the hardships she had faced alone. He finally understood the true depth of her strength a strength forged not in grand, dramatic moments, but in the quiet, daily acts of love and sacrifice.

That evening, they found themselves in his temporary office. It was a space they had avoided a room that once represented the cold, corporate stranger he had been when he first arrived. But now, it felt different. Holly had brought over a pot of her grandmother's beef stew, its rich, savory aroma filling the sterile space and transforming it into something that, for the first time, felt like a place someone could actually live in. They sat on the floor, their backs against the wall, eating from warm ceramic bowls, the town's master plan spread out around them like a beautiful, chaotic picnic blanket.

"You were so brave," Noel said, breaking the comfortable silence. He had been replaying her story in his mind all day. "I was running around a city of millions, thinking my problems were so big. And you were here, quietly holding a whole world together."

"We all do what we have to do," she said softly, though she accepted his words with a small, grateful smile. She looked at him then, her eyes full of deep, empathetic curiosity. "You told me you were scared," she said gently. "And that you were chasing something. But you never really told me what it was like day to day. What really happened to that boy who loved sketching on the bridge?"

Noel set his empty bowl aside. He leaned his head back against the wall, staring up at the acoustic tile ceiling as if he could see the last ten years projected there. He had given her the headlines of his story; now, he owed her the fine print.

"He got lost," Noel began, his voice a low, introspective rumble. "He got to this huge, famous school of architecture and realized, very quickly, that he was completely out of his depth. It was more than just being a small-town kid it was a whole different language. I was used to thinking about how a building would feel, how it would serve the people inside it. They were all talking about deconstructionist theory and semiotics. They spoke in a code I didn't understand."

He paused, then recounted a specific, searing memory from his first semester. "My first major design critique," he said, a humorless smile touching his lips. "The project was a small public pavilion. Sound familiar?"

Holly's hand found his on the floor, giving it a gentle squeeze.

"I basically drew a simplified version of our holly-leaf pavilion. I talked about creating a sense of community, of shelter. I used the word *heart* in my presentation." He let out a short, sharp laugh. "The professor a famous architect who designed buildings that all looked like angry robots completely eviscerated me. He called my design 'painfully sentimental,' 'theoretically unsophisticated,' and 'devoid of any architectural courage.' He said I was decorating, not designing."

The memory was still raw, even a decade later. "I was humiliated. I felt like the biggest, most naïve fool in the world. So I made a decision I was never going to be that sentimental kid again. I checked out every book on architectural theory from the library. I learned the code. I learned how to talk about 'juxtaposition' and 'liminal spaces.' I learned how to design angry robots. And I buried the boy who sketched on the bridge so deep, I wasn't sure he still existed."

His story shifted from the university to the city itself. "Then came the internship, and the job, and Amelia," he said, finally naming the ghost from his past. "She was… the personification of the world I was trying to conquer. Brilliant, driven, and completely unsentimental. Our relationship was like a business partnership. We'd go to networking events, critique each other's proposals. We were a power couple. It was exciting. It felt like winning."

He described the intoxicating thrill of his first big, successful project the chrome reindeer. "I poured everything I had into that," he admitted. "The technical challenge was immense. The budget was huge. And when we unveiled it, the praise, the articles, the bonuses… it was a drug, Holly. A powerful one. For a while, that applause was loud enough to drown out the silence in my own life. It was loud enough to drown out the guilt I felt every time I thought of you, of the promise I was breaking with every new success."

But the high, like any drug, began to fade, leaving only a hollow ache. "The emptiness set in about three years ago," he said quietly. "I was at this incredibly lavish launch party for a new boutique hotel I'd designed. It was on a rooftop overlooking the city. Everyone was telling me I was a genius, champagne was flowing… and I felt nothing. I was completely disconnected. It was like I was watching a movie of my life, and I wasn't even the main character. I was just a special effect."

He had gone home that night to his vast, empty apartment with its panoramic view and had tried, for the first time in years, to sketch for fun. "I pulled out a sketchbook, a real one, with paper. And I just… couldn't. My hands, which used to know what to do, just felt clumsy. My head, once full of fantastical ideas, was now filled with client feedback and budget constraints. My creativity wasn't mine anymore it belonged to my firm. The joy was gone. All that was left were the bones."

That was when he had started running from his past. "I stopped reading your mom's Christmas letters," he confessed, shame tightening his voice. "I'd ignore my dad's calls if I thought he was going to talk about Evergreen Hollow. Every reminder of this place was a reminder of what I'd lost in myself. It reminded me of the boy who could design a gingerbread clocktower without worrying about its structural integrity. And that reminder was too painful. I wasn't just leaving you behind, Holly. I was leaving the best version of myself behind, and I couldn't bear to look back and see how far I'd gone."

He finally turned to look at her, his eyes full of a decade's worth of loneliness. "So, when Mayor Thompson called," he said, bringing the story full circle, "my first reaction was pure arrogance. A small-town contest? It was beneath me. But then… he said the name of the town. And it was like a key turning in a lock I'd forgotten was even there. A deeper part of me the part that was so tired of angry robots and empty apartments saw it as a lifeline."

He reached out and took her hand, his grip tight with desperate sincerity. "I didn't come back to save the town,

Holly. I think, deep down, I came back hoping the town could save me. I came back to see if that boy the one who sketched with you on the bridge was still in here somewhere."

Holly's heart ached for him for the scared, lonely boy who had gotten so lost in the wilderness of his own ambition. She brought his hand to her cheek, holding it there.

"He's still in there, Noel," she whispered, her voice a soothing balm over his raw, open wounds. "I've seen him. He's in the beautiful, thoughtful blueprints you drew for Arthur's frames. He's in the stubborn, brilliant way you figured out how to fix the town's generator. And he was definitely in that barn at Blackwood Pines, laughing about that stupid netting machine." She leaned in and pressed a soft, gentle kiss to his lips. "He never really left. He was just waiting for you to come home."

They sat in silence for a long time, the last of the unsaid finally spoken, the last gaps in their history finally filled. They knew each other now, completely. They had seen the scars, the fears, and the quiet, lonely battles the other had fought.

Their gazes drifted to the master plan spread out on the floor the beautiful, chaotic map of their shared future. The Evergreen Gala. The final, grand expression of their journey. Their purpose now felt clearer and more profound than ever. It wasn't about the prize money. It wasn't about beating Pine Ridge. It wasn't even about healing their own past anymore.

It was about giving the town a celebration worthy of its story a story of endurance, community, and quiet strength. A story that, they now realized, was so much like their own.

They had faced all their ghosts. Now, they were ready to face the final challenge together not as two people healing, but as one solid, unbreakable whole.

Chapter 23

The London Call

The day before the Evergreen Gala was the most perfect day Evergreen Hollow had seen in a decade. A fresh, six-inch blanket of snow had fallen overnight, and now the sun was out brilliant in a cloudless, sapphire-blue sky making the entire town glitter as if it had been dusted with diamonds. The air was cold, crisp, and filled with the joyful, chaotic sounds of a town on the verge of triumph.

Main Street was a whirlwind of happy, purposeful activity. Volunteers carefully hung the last of the hand-painted signs. Zara directed a group of teenagers weaving fresh, fragrant pine boughs into garlands around the lampposts. Arthur Vance, looking almost cheerful, was putting the finishing touches on the last of his magnificent Memory Lane frames. At the center of it all, the Community Canvas was a breathtaking explosion of color a vibrant, chaotic, and deeply moving testament to the town's collective heart. The project was no longer a plan on paper; it was a living, breathing entity, and its success felt as bright and certain as the winter sun.

The heart of this new energy was Holly and Noel. They moved through the happy chaos as a single, seamless unit, their love for each other an open secret that seemed to fuel the town's optimism. They were a team in the deepest sense of the word, and everyone could see it. They shared a quick, laughing kiss behind the towering town Christmas tree a private moment in a public space that felt like a promise. Later, across the bustling square, their eyes met, and they shared a look of such profound love and shared accomplishment that Mrs. Gable, who witnessed it, had to dab at her eyes with a handkerchief.

They were standing by the newly constructed warming hut, admiring how the high school woodshop class had perfectly executed their combined design, when Noel's phone began to ring a sharp, intrusive sound in the festive air.

He glanced at the screen, and the easy smile on his face tightened almost imperceptibly. The caller ID read *Marcus Thorne* his boss, the architect of his glittering, empty life in Chicago.

"I should probably take this," he said to Holly, his voice carefully neutral. "I'll be right back." He gave her hand a quick, reassuring squeeze and stepped away, seeking the relative quiet of the narrow alleyway that ran alongside The Rolling Pin. He didn't want this intrusion from his old life to break the perfect, magical spell of the day.

Holly watched him go, a small, uneasy flicker rising in her chest. She turned her attention back to the volunteers, directing a pair of them on the best way to hang a wreath on the hut's door. But her senses were on high alert. She couldn't hear the voice on the other end of the line, but she could see him and she could hear the clipped, tense cadence of his own responses drifting out into the cold air.

"Marcus," Noel said, his back to Main Street, his voice a low murmur. "Now's not a good time. I'm in the middle of something."

He listened, his body growing more rigid. Holly saw him run a hand through his hair a gesture of stress and agitation she was beginning to recognize. It was the gesture of the Chicago architect, not the Evergreen Hollow man she had fallen in love with all over again.

"What?" he said, his voice sharp with disbelief. "London? In two days? That's… that's impossible, Marcus. The final presentation isn't for another month."

Holly froze, a string of fairy lights slipping from her grasp. *London.* The word was a foreign planet, a distant, glittering world that had nothing to do with this small, perfect snow globe of a day.

Noel paced in the narrow alley, a short, agitated back-and-forth. He was a caged animal. "I understand the scale of this," he said, his voice tight with tension that carried all the way to where Holly stood. "Of course I do. It's the biggest project of my career the one we've been chasing for a year."

The biggest project of his career. The phrase landed in Holly's heart like a stone. Bigger than this. More important than this. More important than her. The old, familiar fear the one she thought she had finally conquered came rushing back, cold and sickening. The fear that this small town, that *she*, would never be enough to compete with the big, shiny world that had claimed him once before.

"But the timing is insane," Noel said, his voice a low, desperate argument. "The Gala is tomorrow. I can't just drop everything here. People are depending on me."

To Holly's ears, it didn't sound like a refusal. It sounded like a logistical complaint a man trying to solve a scheduling problem, not a man making a choice of the heart. Her world, so bright and full of color moments before, began to fade around the edges. The happy sounds of the town dulled into a distant hum. All she could focus on was the tense silhouette of the man she loved, being pulled away from her by a voice she couldn't hear.

And then came the final, fatal line.

"Look," Noel said, his voice full of weary frustration. "Let me... let me see what I can do. I need to think. I'll call you back."

He hung up the phone. *Let me see what I can do.* The words were a death sentence. To Holly, they meant only one thing: he was going to try. He was going to try and leave. Just like last time. The lost letter had proven their first breakup was a tragic misunderstanding. But this this was a choice. He was standing at a crossroads, and from everything she had just seen and heard, he was choosing the path that led away from her.

The old wound the one she thought had finally healed ripped open again, raw and agonizing.

Noel stood in the alley for a long moment, his mind a whirlwind. *London.* The opportunity of a lifetime. The validation he had once craved more than anything. He looked at the phone in his hand, then thought of Holly of the warmth in her eyes, of the life they were just beginning to build. The choice, he realized with stunning clarity, wasn't a choice at all. There was no choice. There was only Holly.

He took a deep breath, a decision settling in his soul, and turned back to her to tell her everything, to laugh with her about the absurdity of his boss's timing.

But she was already there, just outside the alley, her face a pale, frozen mask of heartbreak. The joy that had animated her features all day was gone, replaced by a devastating, quiet resignation he recognized all too well. It was the look she'd worn the day he first arrived back in town.

He knew instantly that something was terribly wrong.

"Holly?" he said, his voice full of dread. "What is it? What's wrong?"

"London," she said, the single word a shard of ice. It wasn't a question it was an accusation. "I heard you talking. It's the biggest project of your career."

"Holly, wait," he said, stepping toward her, his hands outstretched. "It's not what you think. My boss just… he doesn't understand what's happening here."

"Oh, I think I understand perfectly," she said, her voice brittle and fragile, close to breaking. "I heard you. You said you'd 'see what you can do.' I know what that means, Noel. It means you're looking for a way a way to leave. Isn't it?"

"No! That's not what I meant," he protested, desperation sharpening his tone. "I was just trying to get him off the phone!"

"Were you?" she asked, a single tear tracing down her cold cheek. "It's always the same, isn't it? There will always be a bigger project, a shinier city, a more important call to take. And I… I'll always be here, in this small town, with my small life. I can't compete with London, Noel. I finally understand that."

"This isn't a competition!" he pleaded, his voice ragged. "This isn't the same as before! Everything's different now!"

"Is it?" she whispered, the fight draining out of her, replaced by a deep, weary sadness. She looked at him, her eyes full of a decade of recycled pain hurt so deep it had become part of her. "Some things never change. You should go. It's what you're good at."

Before he could find the words before he could scream that he was choosing *her* she had already turned away. She didn't run. She walked, with slow, deliberate finality, away from the joyful chaos of the town square, away from the dream they had rebuilt, and disappeared through the door that led up to her apartment.

She left him standing alone in the alley, the weight of her words and of their entire history crashing down upon him. He looked at the phone in his hand, the dark, silent screen that connected him to a life he no longer wanted. Then he looked at the empty doorway she had just walked through the entrance to the only life he did.

In the distance, he could hear the volunteer band practicing a cheerful Christmas carol for the Gala a celebration of the very hope and unity he had just, in one terrible, misunderstood moment, destroyed. He had a choice to make, a call to return. But in Holly's eyes, he had already made it.

Chapter 24

Some Things Never Change

Holly's apartment, which only hours before had been a sanctuary of shared peace and burgeoning love, was now a cage. The silence was the most unbearable part a thick, suffocating blanket that amplified the frantic, broken rhythm of her thoughts. She moved through the small rooms with mechanical, restless energy, straightening cushions already straight, wiping down counters already clean. Every object felt like a fresh betrayal. The two coffee mugs by the sink. The charcoal sketch they had been working on for the Gala's program cover, left unfinished on the kitchen table. His coat, forgotten in his haste to take the call, still hung over the back of a chair the faint, clean scent of him lingering like a cruel ghost.

She had been a fool. A naïve, sentimental fool. She had allowed herself to believe this time was different that he was different. The last few weeks, which had felt like a beautiful, impossible dream, now seemed like a cruel joke. She had let him in, torn down every wall she had so carefully built over the last ten years, only for him to prove that her oldest fear the one that had protected her for so long was the only truth she should have trusted.

Some things never change.

The phrase echoed in her mind like a bitter mantra. An

opportunity calls, a bigger, shinier world beckons, and Noel Bishop leaves. It was the unchanging physics of their shared universe.

She found herself in her small bedroom, pulling open the bottom drawer of her dresser. Beneath a pile of old sweaters was the wooden box containing her sketchbooks the ones she and Noel had looked through with such joy. She opened it but didn't look at their shared designs. Instead, she dug deeper, pulling out a sketchbook from years ago, from the height of her loneliness after her grandmother had passed.

She flipped through the pages. They were filled not with fantastical buildings but with stark, lonely landscapes of Evergreen Hollow in winter leafless trees, empty streets, a dark, frozen river. It was the work of a woman who had accepted that her world was small, quiet, and safe.

This was who she was, she thought, her heart a cold, heavy stone in her chest. She wasn't a woman who belonged in London. She belonged to these quiet, solitary landscapes.

A sharp, insistent knock on her door made her jump. Her first wild thought was Noel but she knew it wasn't. He would have just left.

She opened the door to find Zara standing there, her face a mask of fierce concern, holding a container that smelled unmistakably like macaroni and cheese.

"You're not answering your phone," Zara said, skipping any greeting as she marched into the kitchen. "I saw you walk away. I saw his face. Spill. Now."

Holly shook her head, exhaustion washing over her. "There's nothing to spill. It's over."

"Over?" Zara scoffed, pulling two forks from a drawer. "You were 'over' for ten years, Holly. What we've seen these past few weeks is the opposite of over. What happened?"

"He's leaving," Holly said flatly. "He got a call. A big, career-making project in London. He's going."

Zara froze, her fork hovering midair. "He told you that? He said, 'Holly, I'm leaving for London'?"

"He didn't have to," Holly snapped, the old pain sharpening her tone. "I heard him. I saw him. It's the biggest project of his career, Zara. How am I supposed to compete with that? How is this town supposed to compete with that?"

"So, you didn't even talk to him? You just ran?" Zara challenged, her usual teasing gone, replaced with tough, loving firmness. "Did you ask him if he was going? Did you give him a chance to explain?"

"I heard what I heard!" Holly insisted, her voice rising. "He said he'd 'see what he could do.' It's the same thing all over again! I can't go through that again, Zara. I won't."

"Go through what, exactly?" Zara pressed, stepping closer. "Because the Noel Bishop who's been here for the past month is not the teenage boy who left for college. The man I've seen has fought for you. He's championed your ideas. He stood up to Frank Henderson. He went into a freezing basement and brought the town's power back on with you. He looks at you like you're the only thing in the world. Are you really going to throw that away because of half a phone call you overheard in an alley?"

"You don't understand," Holly whispered, her defenses beginning to crumble.

"Oh, I understand perfectly," Zara said, her voice softening. "You're terrified. And you're letting a ghost from ten years ago make your decisions for you. The hurt is real, I get that. But the man who's here now is real, too. And you're not the same girl he left. You're the woman who saved this bakery the woman who's saving this town. Are you really going to let him go without a fight? Without even asking him the question?"

Holly just stared at her best friend, tears welling in her eyes. Zara's words were a mirror brutal, but necessary. She had reacted not as the strong, capable woman she'd become, but as the heartbroken girl she used to be.

But was she still that girl?

Noel sat in the sterile silence of his temporary office, the joyful sounds of the town outside reduced to a muffled, mocking hum. He stared at the dark screen of his phone as if it were venomous. Holly's final words *"You should go. It's what you're good at."* played on a relentless loop in his mind.

How could she think that? After everything they had shared the confessions, the collaboration, the kisses how could she believe he would just walk away? The injustice of it burned in his throat, bitter and raw. It felt as if all their trust, all their healing, had been nothing but a fragile illusion shattered by the first gust of wind from his old life.

A self-destructive thought crept in. *Maybe she's right.* Maybe it would be easier to leave. He could get on a plane, throw himself into the London project, and bury his heartbreak under a mountain of blueprints and deadlines. It was familiar. It was safe. It was what he was good at.

He was staring blankly at the wall when a soft knock came at the door. He ignored it. It came again, more insistent this time. With a groan, he got up and opened it. His father stood there, holding two steaming mugs.

"Your mother sent over some of her mulled cider," his dad said, his calm eyes taking in the bleak room and his son's despair. "Figured you could use it."

Noel took the mug. The warm, spicy scent was a sudden, aching reminder of a thousand childhood Christmases. His father came in and sat on the edge of the folding table, saying nothing at first just *being there.*

"Something's wrong with you and Holly," his dad said finally not as a question, but as a quiet truth.

That simple empathy undid him. The story poured out London, the misunderstanding, Holly's words, his heartbreak.

His father listened patiently. When Noel finished, he didn't offer easy advice. He just looked at his son the successful architect, the man who had built a life far from home and saw the boy still trying to prove himself.

"You've spent a good part of your life trying to prove you're not that small-town kid anymore," his dad said gently. "You built this big, impressive career to prove it to the world, to your colleagues, maybe even to Holly." He took a sip of cider. "But who were you really trying to prove it to? Seems to me, the only person who still thinks that boy from Evergreen Hollow wasn't good enough... is you."

The words hit Noel like a blow.

"You came back here," his father continued, "and you found something real. You found a purpose that has nothing to do with budgets or buildings. You found that boy again the one who likes to build things that matter. The one who loves that girl." His gaze held firm. "Your success was never supposed to be about *buildings,* son. It was supposed to be about *building a life.* Are you going to let some blueprint in a city you don't even like tear down the foundation of the life you've just started building right here?"

After his father left, Noel sat in silence, the warm mug cradled in his hands, his father's words echoing through the room.

The only person who thinks that boy wasn't good enough is you.

He looked at his tablet screen the rendering of the Town Hall projection, his technical structure supporting her magical story. His whole career had been one long overcompensation for the insecurity he'd carried from this town.

He didn't need to prove anything anymore. London wasn't a dream. It was just a job and one he no longer wanted.

He finally understood what *home* was. It wasn't a place you earned the right to return to. It was the place that reminded you what was worth fighting for.

Holly stood by her apartment window, looking down at the Community Canvas. In the twilight, she could see the section they had painted together the night before the place where her deep red blended into his twilight blue.

Zara was right. She wasn't the same girl who had been broken by a phone call ten years ago. She was a woman who had built a life, fought for her town, and faced her ghosts. She had been waiting for Noel to prove he wouldn't leave, when all along, she had the power to fight for him to stay.

Noel sat in his office, his decision suddenly, stunningly clear. His ambition had been a map that led him into a wilderness of his own making. Holly had been his North Star the way home.

Holly pulled on her coat, her face set with fierce determination. She was done waiting. She was going to find him. She was going to fight for *them.*

Noel picked up his phone, his thumb hovering over the screen. He scrolled past his boss's name the London call already a thing of the past and found hers. His heart ached with desperate, hopeful love.

He knew what he had to do.

He had to prove her wrong.

He had to prove that some things the most important things *do* change.

People change.

And he had, finally, come home.

Chapter 25

The Door That Always Closes

Holly ran. She didn't know where she was going only that she had to move. The fierce, righteous determination that had propelled her from her apartment just moments before had curdled into frantic, desperate panic. Zara's words, her father-in-law's wisdom, her own epiphany it all felt like a foolish, naïve dream in the face of the cold, hard reality she believed she had just discovered.

She arrived at Noel's temporary office, her heart hammering against her ribs, her carefully prepared speech now a jumble in her throat. She pushed the door open without knocking. The room was empty.

A single, harsh fluorescent light hummed overhead, illuminating a scene of quiet abandonment. The desk was clear, save for his tablet and a few stray papers. The large town map, once covered in their combined notes and colored pins, was now bare, wiped clean. An empty coffee cup sat beside a crumpled napkin. The space had been vacated. He was already gone or at least, he had begun erasing himself.

Her gaze fell on the tablet, its screen still glowing. She shouldn't look. It would be a violation of his privacy a betrayal of the fragile trust they had rebuilt. But she couldn't stop herself. She was a moth drawn to a flame she knew would burn her. With a trembling hand, she touched the screen.

It was an email, half-composed. The recipient was Marcus Thorne. The subject line read simply: **London.** The body contained only a few clipped, agonizingly ambiguous words:

"Marcus,

Regarding the call I need to make some arrangements here first. Things are more complicated than I anticipated."

Holly felt the air leave her lungs, a silent, painful punch to the gut. *Arrangements. Complicated.* It wasn't a no. It was a calculation. The language of a man quietly preparing an exit strategy. Her mind, now fertile ground for worst-case scenarios, filled in the blanks. The "complication" was her. The "arrangements" were his polite, efficient way of extracting himself from her life before moving on to the next, bigger thing.

The seed of doubt that Zara had planted the fragile hope that she might have been wrong withered and died. Her fear, it turned out, had been right all along. It had been the only thing telling her the truth. She backed out of the room, a strangled sob caught in her throat, the afterimage of the email burned into her mind.

Meanwhile, Noel moved with the clarity and purpose of a man who had finally found his North Star. His conversation with his father had been a key, turning the lock on a decade of self-doubt. His glittering career had been a misguided attempt to prove his worth. He didn't need to prove it anymore he just needed to live it.

He drove to his parents' house, where he'd been staying, and walked straight to the guest room that had once been his childhood bedroom. He pulled out a single, medium-sized duffel bag. He didn't pack his suits or his architectural tools. Instead, he packed the things that represented the boy from Evergreen Hollow an old, worn copy of his favorite book, a faded photograph of him and Holly on the Old Town Bridge, and a soft gray sweater his mother had knit years ago, the one Holly had always loved to borrow. It wasn't a bag for a trip to London. It was a bag for a man who was finally, truly, coming home.

His plan was simple. Words were not enough he had learned that the hard way. He needed to show her. He would go to the bakery, find her, and in front of her, call Marcus Thorne to officially and unequivocally resign from the firm. He would burn the bridge to his old life, leaving no doubt, no escape route. It would be a grand gesture, yes but after a decade of silence and a week of turmoil, it was the only thing loud and clear enough to silence her fears.

He arrived at *The Rolling Pin*, the duffel bag feeling both heavy and impossibly light in his hand. The front of the bakery was dark, the chairs stacked on the tables. The **Closed** sign hung in the window. He called her name into the quiet, fragrant space, but there was no answer.

Of course. She would be upstairs in her apartment. His heart quickened. He looked at the door to the internal staircase the one he had never gone through. It felt like crossing a final, intimate threshold. He knew he should probably go outside and knock on her apartment's front door, but a desperate, romantic urgency propelled him forward. He wanted to fix this now to erase the hurt from her face and replace it with the certainty of his choice.

He took a step toward the stairs, the bag in his hand, his speech rehearsed, his heart full of desperate, hopeful love.

And at that exact moment, the front door of the bakery burst open, the bell chiming a frantic, panicked tune.

Holly stood there, silhouetted against the streetlights, her face pale, her eyes wide and haunted. She had clearly been running. She saw him, and for a fleeting second, desperate hope flashed in her eyes. Then her gaze dropped to the duffel bag at his feet.

And in an instant, everything changed. The hope died, replaced by a look of such profound heartbreak that it knocked the wind out of him.

He saw it all unfold in slow motion the empty office, the email she must have read, and now this: the final, irrefutable proof. The man she loved, standing in the heart of her world, with a packed bag in his hand, ready to leave.

"So, it's true," she said, her voice hollow, broken all the fire gone. "You're leaving."

"Holly, no," he said, his voice desperate, panicked. He dropped the bag as if it were burning, stepping toward her. "Wait. This isn't what you think. I packed this for I was coming to tell you"

But she was no longer listening. She was trapped in the agonizing loop of her own deepest pain, the story she had been telling herself for ten years finally reaching its terrible conclusion.

"To tell me what?" she interrupted, her voice trembling, a bitter shell forming around her heart. "That you're sorry? That it's a wonderful opportunity, but the timing is terrible? I've heard it before, Noel. I don't need to hear it again. Please, just… don't."

"You're not listening to me!" he cried, heartbreak and frustration mounting. He felt like he was shouting from behind a wall of glass. "I packed this bag to leave my old life behind not to leave you!"

Her face crumpled, the pain too much to bear. "I can't do this," she whispered, shaking her head and stepping back, away from the future he was trying to offer. "I can't stand here and watch you walk out that door again. I won't." She looked at the front door of the bakery her door and her expression was one of pure agony. "It's the door that always closes, Noel. It was always going to close. And I can't… I can't watch it happen one more time."

And then, to protect herself from the one thing she could not bear, she did the only thing she could. Before he could stop her, before he could make his grand gesture, before he could scream that she was wrong, she turned.

She walked back to the front door of her bakery her home, her heart. She pulled it open and, without looking back, stepped out into the cold and shut it behind her.

The gentle chime of the bell was the most sorrowful sound Noel had ever heard.

He stood in the ringing silence, in the warm, fragrant heart of her world, completely, utterly alone. He was holding the proof of his commitment the symbol of his final choice and it had been misinterpreted as the ultimate act of betrayal. He looked at the door she had just closed the door that had separated them for a decade, the door that always closes.

But this time, she had been the one to close it.

The Evergreen Gala the town's great celebration of hope and unity was tomorrow. But as Noel stood alone in the darkness, he knew he had already lost the one thing that made any of it matter at all.

Part 3

The Fire

Chapter 26

A Packed Suitcase, An Empty Feeling

The gentle chime of the bell as the bakery door closed was the loudest sound Noel had ever heard. It was a sound of absolute finality an exclamation point at the end of a ten-year-long, tragic sentence. He was left standing in the sudden, profound silence of Holly's world a world he was no longer a part of.

He stood there for a long time, unmoving, the duffel bag a lead weight at his feet. The warm, fragrant air that had once been his sanctuary now felt suffocating, each scent a specific and painful memory. The rich aroma of chocolate recalled their late-night work sessions the ghost of their almost-kiss. The sharp, sweet scent of cinnamon carried the memory of her laughter. The yeasty, wholesome smell of baking bread was the scent of the life he had just, in one catastrophically misunderstood moment, lost completely.

Her grandmother's clock ticked on the wall, each sound a tiny hammer blow against his fractured heart. Tick-tock. A countdown to the Gala the supposed culmination of their shared victory, which now felt like a funeral procession. Tick-tock. A measure of the seconds, minutes, and hours he would have to live with the image of her face shattered with a pain he had inadvertently caused.

He replayed the scene in his mind, desperately searching for the exact moment it had all gone wrong. The packed bag. The empty office. The half-written email. It was a perfect storm of circumstantial evidence a prosecutor's dream of a case against him and he'd been given no chance to mount a defense. A surge of hot, helpless anger rose in him at the injustice of it all, at the sheer, tragic cruelty of their timing. But just as quickly, the anger gave way to a wave of crushing despair. Maybe they were cursed. Maybe the ghost of their first mistake was too powerful to ever truly be exorcised, destined to repeat itself in different, ever more painful ways.

He couldn't stay here. This was her space, her heart, and he was now a trespasser. He picked up the duffel bag the symbol of his failed grand gesture and walked out, the bell chiming his departure into the cold, empty night.

He didn't go to his parents' house. Instead, he drove his movements numb and automatic back to the scenic overlook above town. He got out of the car and walked to the stone wall, the wind cold and sharp against his face. Below him, Evergreen Hollow glittered, a perfect jewel-box town preparing for its big moment. Every light that glowed from the golden warmth of the bridge to the festive strings in the town square was a testament to the work they had done together. The town was a living blueprint of their partnership, and he had just been fired from the project. He was an outsider again, looking in.

He pulled out his phone. The screen was dark, but he knew the unanswered call and the unreturned text from Marcus were waiting for him a portal to another world, another life, an escape route. For a bitter moment, he considered it. He could call Marcus back, get on the first plane to London, and bury this heartbreak under a mountain of work. It was what he was good at, after all. He could disappear. He could become the ghost she already thought he was.

But he knew with a certainty that cut through his despair that it would be a life sentence: a lifetime of quiet, empty apartments and meaningless, soulless projects; a lifetime of wondering what could have been. He couldn't do it. He hadn't come this far, hadn't found himself again, only to run away when it got hard.

With a steady hand, he dialed.

"Bishop," Marcus Thorne's voice barked through the phone, impatient and laced with static. "It's about time. I've got you booked on the 6 a.m. out of Burlington. The presentation is everything. Don't tell me you're getting sentimental over some small-town Christmas pageant."

Noel looked down at the glittering town the place that held every important piece of his life. He thought of Holly's face, the feel of her hand in his, the taste of their last, perfect kiss.

"I am," Noel said, his voice surprisingly calm and clear in the cold, windy night. "I'm getting sentimental."

"What?" Marcus sputtered, incredulous.

"I'm not coming, Marcus," Noel said the words feeling like the first truly honest ones he had spoken in his professional life. "Not to London. Not back to Chicago. I'm staying here."

"Are you insane?" Marcus's voice rose, a mixture of disbelief and fury. "This is the Kensington project! This is the one that gets your name on the cover of every architectural magazine on the planet! You're throwing that away for… what? For a bunch of lumberjacks and some Christmas lights?"

"I'm throwing that away for a life," Noel said simply. "For a chance to build something that actually matters. I am officially resigning from the firm, Marcus effective immediately."

The silence on the other end of the line was frigid. "You'll be blacklisted, Bishop," Marcus finally hissed, his voice cold with rage. "I'll make sure of it. You'll never work on a major project in this industry again."

A year ago, that threat would have sent a chill of pure terror down his spine. Tonight, it was strangely liberating. The bars of his gilded cage were melting away.

"I'm counting on it," Noel said, and before Marcus could reply, he ended the call.

He stood there, phone in hand, a quiet, terrifying freedom washing over him. He had done it. He had burned the bridge to his old life. He had made his choice irrevocably. But the elation he expected didn't come. Because although he had made the choice, he had still lost the one person it was all for.

He drove to his parents' house, the duffel bag sitting in the passenger seat like a silent, mocking companion. He walked into the warm, familiar kitchen and found his father sitting at the table, reading the local paper, a cup of tea steaming beside him. His father looked up, took one look at his son's face, and folded the newspaper.

"That bad?" he asked quietly.

And for the second time in his life, Noel sat at his childhood kitchen table and confessed his heartbreak. He told his father everything the terrible misunderstanding, the packed bag, Holly closing the door on him, and the phone call he had just made.

"I did it, Dad," he said, his voice thick with both pride and despair. "I finally chose. I quit. I'm staying. And in the process, I've lost her for good. She'll never believe me now."

His father listened, his gaze steady and kind. When Noel finished, he rose and poured his son a cup of tea.

"You two..." his dad said, his voice a low, thoughtful rumble as he sat back down. "You're like a fire that's been smothered under wet leaves for ten years. All that time, there was heat but no light, no warmth. Just smoke. Now you've finally gotten a flame going. It's bright and beautiful, but it's new. And what you've just had this fight it's like a big gust of wind. It's kicked up all the old ash and smoke from the last ten years. Right now, it stings the eyes. You can't see clearly. She can't see clearly."

He leaned forward, his expression earnest. "You can't fix this with quiet words, son. You can't fix it by explaining about a packed bag. A misunderstanding this big, a hurt this old you have to fight it with something bigger. You need a gesture so bright, so loud, and so undeniable that it burns away all that smoke and ash for good. You have to give her a fire she can't ignore."

His father's words the metaphor of the fire sparked something in Noel's exhausted mind. A new idea. A desperate, impossible, absolutely necessary plan. He couldn't just tell Holly he was staying. He had to show her. He had to show the entire town. He had to build something.

He stood up, a manic, brilliant energy surging through him, chasing away the despair. "The Pavilion," he said, his voice a hoarse whisper. "The Evergreen Project."

It wasn't about winning the contest anymore. It was about winning her. He would take their oldest, most sacred dream the holly-leaf pavilion and make part of it real. Right now. Overnight.

He raced back to his office, the mind of a world-class architect now fully unleashed on the most important project of his life. He grabbed the old sketch the one he carried with him like a prayer and spread it out on the table. The full pavilion was impossible overnight. But the archway the magnificent archway shaped like two intersecting holly leaves that he could build.

He was no longer despairing. He was a man on a mission. He grabbed his phone, his fingers flying across the screen. He wasn't calling clients in London; he was calling every 24-hour lumber supplier and steel fabricator within a hundred-mile radius. He was calling in favors from old college friends who owed him. He was texting the lead of the professional crew he'd hired, offering them triple time for an all-night job.

He stood in the sterile office, his face illuminated by the glow of his tablet a designer who had finally, truly found his purpose. He wasn't just building an archway. He was building a grand gesture. He was building an apology. He was building a beacon to guide her home.

The packed suitcase sat forgotten in the corner. Its purpose had failed, but it had led him here. And the feeling in his chest was no longer empty it was full of a terrifying, brilliant, all-consuming fire.

Chapter 27

The Sound of A Closing Door

The sound of the bell on the bakery door her own departure echoed in Holly's ears long after she had fled. She didn't go far. She ended up on the small wrought-iron bench in the park behind the town hall, the one where she had told Noel about her grandmother's legacy. The night was cold, the air so still she could hear the faint, happy sounds of last-minute Gala preparations drifting from the town square. It sounded like a party in another universe.

She sat there, huddled in her coat, a profound and hollow numbness spreading through her. She had done it. She had protected herself. The door had been about to close to slam shut on her heart just as it had ten years ago and she had simply walked through it first. It was a strange, bitter kind of victory. The pain was immense, a deep, crushing ache in her chest, but the terrible, gut-wrenching uncertainty was finally over. She had taken control. She had ended it on her own terms before he could.

She told herself this over and over, a desperate litany against the rising tide of regret. He had a packed bag. He had an empty office. He had an email about London on his screen. The evidence was irrefutable. She had done the only logical, self-preserving thing she could do.

But as the hours ticked by on the illuminated town clock, the cold seeping into her bones, her certainty began to fray. The image of his face when she had turned away the sheer, wounded shock, the desperate denial kept replaying in her mind. He hadn't looked like a man executing a clean exit strategy. He had looked like a man watching his entire world collapse.

"Did you even ask him?" Zara's voice a persistent, rational ghost in the fog of her pain began to whisper in her ear. "Are you going to let a ghost from ten years ago make your decisions for you?"

She had been so sure, so certain that history was repeating itself. But was it? The Noel who had stood in her bakery was not the ambitious, scared boy from a decade ago. He was the man who had looked at her with such raw honesty in her apartment and confessed his deepest fears. He was the man who had held her hand on the bridge and promised her a future. He was the man who had looked at her with awe and called her magic. Could that man this new, solid, present man really just pack a bag and walk away?

The question was a tiny crack in the icy wall of her certainty. And through it, a terrifying, alternative possibility began to seep in. What if she was wrong? What if the packed bag, the empty office, the email… what if it was all just another tragic, catastrophic misunderstanding? The thought was so agonizing so full of a regret far deeper than the pain of being left that she pushed it down, burying it under the cold, hard weight of her fear. It was safer to believe he had left. It was safer to be the victim than the one who had made the gravest mistake of her life.

She didn't sleep. She spent the night on her sofa, wrapped in a blanket, watching the snow fall outside her window. The night was a long, silent vigil for a love she had just sentenced to death.

The morning of the Evergreen Gala dawned gray and overcast, the sky the color of unpolished silver. The town, however, was oblivious to her personal tragedy. It was electric with joy and anticipation that felt, to Holly, like a physical assault. The sound of cheerful Christmas music, the laughter of children, the happy shouts of volunteers it was all a mocking counterpoint to the profound silence in her heart.

She went down to the bakery, her movements slow and automatic, her face a pale, tired mask. She baked out of pure muscle memory, her hands going through the familiar motions while her mind was a million miles away.

Zara found her there, her usual boisterous energy subdued by the visible cloud of misery hanging over her best friend.

"Holly," she said gently, expertly piping icing onto a tray of gingerbread men. "You look like you haven't slept in a week. Talk to me."

"There's nothing to say," Holly said, her voice flat. "It's the day of the Gala. I have to work."

"No," Zara said, putting down the piping bag and turning to face her, her expression serious. "You have to live. And right now, you're not living. You're haunting your own bakery. I've been down in the square all morning. So have about a hundred other people. You know who's not there? Noel. No one has seen him since yesterday afternoon. His hired crew is just standing around, waiting for instructions. The Town Hall projection your big, magical finale it's not even set up."

The news sent a fresh wave of sick confirmation through Holly. Of course he wasn't there. He was on a plane. He was gone.

"See?" Holly whispered, her voice cracking. "I told you."

"No, Holly, I don't see," Zara insisted, her voice rising with fierce, loving frustration. "I see a man who's poured his heart and soul into this town, into you, for the past month, who's suddenly vanished the day of the biggest event of his life. That doesn't sound like a man executing a clean getaway. That sounds like a man who is heartbroken."

She took Holly by the shoulders, forcing her to meet her gaze. "You have two choices today, Holly Sutton," she said, her voice low and intense. "You can stand here, hiding behind your apron, and go to that Gala tonight and put on a brave face and pretend to be happy for the town you saved. You can be the lonely, tragic hero of your own sad story. It's the safe choice. No one would blame you."

She gave her a little shake. "Or you can be the bravest you've ever been. You can choose to believe in the man you love the man who has shown you, in a thousand different ways, that he's changed. You can go out there and fight for him. You can fight for the happy ending you both deserve. It's the terrifying choice. It's the one where you might get your heart shattered into a million pieces. But it's the only choice that leads to a life you actually want to live. So, which story are you going to tell your grandkids, Holly? The one where you were safe? Or the one where you were brave?"

Zara's words a brilliant, loving, and brutal distillation of the entire situation struck Holly like a physical blow. She looked at her reflection in the dark glass of the oven door. She saw a tired, heartbroken woman, her eyes red-rimmed, her face pale with grief. She looked like a victim. She looked like the girl who had been left behind.

But that's not who she was.

She was the woman who had held her grandmother's hand through the darkest hours. She was the woman who had kept a legacy alive. She was the woman who had faced down her own fears and the town's skepticism and had built a miracle out of hope and sheer, stubborn will. She was the woman who had fallen in love with Noel Bishop all over again and who, in a moment of pure, unadulterated terror, had slammed the door on their future.

She had been so afraid of the door closing that she had been the one to shut it.

The realization was a painful, clarifying dawn. True strength wasn't found in building walls to protect your heart from pain. It was found in being brave enough to keep the door open, even when you were terrified of who might walk out.

It was late afternoon. The Gala was set to begin in just a few hours. The town was waiting for its leader. Holly looked at Zara her best friend, her rock and a new, fierce, terrified light shone in her eyes.

"Thank you," she whispered, her voice thick with emotion.

She untied her apron the one that had felt like armor all morning and let it fall to the floor. She walked to the hook by the back door and pulled on her coat. Her face was a mask of terrified resolve.

She didn't know where he was. She didn't know if he was even still in town. She didn't know if he would ever forgive her. But she knew she had to try. It was no longer about winning the contest or saving the town. It was about saving the most important thing of all.

She walked out of the bakery and into the festive, expectant crowd not as the architect of their celebration, but as a woman on a desperate, hopeful, and terrifying search for the man she loved.

Chapter 28

A Race Against The Sunrise

The despair that had threatened to swallow Noel whole in the alleyway was a luxury he could no longer afford. As he stood in his parents' kitchen, his father's words about a fire burning away the smoke echoed in his mind, sparking a new, terrifyingly brilliant idea. He was done with words. Done with explanations that could be misunderstood, with gestures that could be misread. He was an architect a builder. He would build his apology. He would build his promise. And he would do it by sunrise.

He left his parents' house a man possessed, a single, impossible goal blazing in his mind: he would build the archway. The grand, soaring, holly-leaf archway that had been the centerpiece of their original Evergreen Project the dream they had sketched together as kids. He would take that piece of their shared soul, that ghost on paper, and make it real. He would plant it in the middle of the town square for Holly and for the whole town to see. It would be an undeniable, structurally sound testament to the fact that he was here to stay.

He had less than twelve hours.

His temporary office became a frantic, high-stakes command center. The first calls were the hardest a test of his conviction.

"Dave, it's Noel Bishop," he said into his phone, his voice sharp and commanding as he paced the small room. He was speaking to the owner of a 24-hour steel fabrication plant in Rutland. "I have an insane, overnight emergency order. I need two ten-meter curved I-beams, and I need them delivered to Evergreen Hollow, Vermont, by 4 a.m. at the latest."

The silence on the other end was thick with disbelief. "Bishop, it's seven o'clock at night. My main crew's gone home. That's an impossible timeline."

"I know it is," Noel said, his voice softening, the corporate commander replaced by a man laying his soul bare. "Look, Dave, I'm not calling as a client. I'm calling as a man who has one chance to fix the biggest mistake of his life and that chance expires at sunrise. I'll pay triple your emergency rate. I'll cover every minute of your crew's overtime. Please. Can you help me?"

Another silence. Then, a weary sigh. "Send me the specs. I'll see what I can do."

One down.

He made the next call to a lumber yard owner his father knew waking the poor man from a deep sleep. He needed the best, driest, most beautiful planks of white oak the man had, and he needed them delivered to the old town mill within the hour. Then came the call to his own hired crew, the small team of professionals who had been helping with the contest. He offered them a bonus so large it made their foreman choke.

"We're building something tonight," Noel told him. "Something that has to be perfect. And it has to be done by dawn."

The final call was the hardest. He called Arthur Vance.

"Vance, it's Noel Bishop," he said, bracing himself.

"It's eight o'clock at night, son. My workshop's closed."

"I know. I need to borrow it or rather, rent it. And your expertise along with it. I'm building something important, and it has to be done tonight."

"You're insane," Arthur grumbled.

"I am," Noel agreed. "But I'm also paying double your daily rate, in cash, for one night's work. And... it's a design that involves a lot of very complex, steam-bent white oak."

A long, considering silence followed. "The old mill has more space," Arthur finally rasped. "Meet me there in thirty minutes. And bring coffee. A lot of it."

By 10 p.m., the vast, cavernous main floor of the old town mill a space that had been silent for a generation was a maelstrom of light, noise, and frantic activity. Temporary floodlights cast long, dancing shadows, making the workers look like giants. The air, thick with the smell of sawdust and ozone from the welders, vibrated with the scream of power saws and the percussive clang of hammers on steel.

Noel was at the center of it all a man transformed. The sleek, polished architect was gone, replaced by a sawdust-covered, grease-stained field marshal leading a desperate charge. His original, tattered sketch of the pavilion was pinned to a board, and his tablet glowed with the complex 3D renderings he'd created on the fly. He was everywhere at once directing the welders as they fused the massive steel I-beams into a foundational arch, consulting with Arthur Vance on the precise curvature for the oak cladding, and working alongside his crew to measure and cut the huge wooden planks.

His father arrived around midnight with a massive thermos of coffee and a bag of sandwiches from the diner. He didn't say much just handed his son a mug, his eyes full of quiet, profound pride. Then he picked up a broom and started sweeping the ever-growing piles of sawdust, a silent, steady presence amid the chaos.

The work became a race, each small victory measured against the relentless ticking of the clock on the wall. The steel frame the great, curving bones of the archway came together with a brutal, industrial grace. Then came the magic the part that was for Holly.

Noel became obsessed with the details. He and Arthur Vance worked side by side at a workbench, their combined expertise a powerful force. Noel had designed a stencil for the delicate, intersecting holly-leaf pattern that was the project's signature. He worked with a router, his hands so used to the sterile glide of a mouse now steady and sure as he carved the familiar, beloved shape into the warm, living wood. Every curve, every point of a leaf, was a word in the apology he couldn't speak a piece of the promise he was desperate to keep.

Around 3 a.m., disaster struck. A crucial support brace, fabricated in Rutland and delivered at great expense, was half an inch too short. It was a tiny error, but on a structure of this scale, it was catastrophic. The entire archway was compromised.

"We're done," one of the welders said, his face grim with exhaustion. "There's no way to fix that. Not tonight."

A wave of cold, black despair washed over Noel. He leaned against the half-finished structure, the steel's chill cutting through the hot shame burning in his chest. He was going to fail. His grand gesture was going to be a half-finished monument to his own hubris.

"Nonsense," a gravelly voice cut through his thoughts. It was Arthur Vance. The old craftsman was studying the problem, his sharp eyes narrowed. "The steel's wrong, so we make the wood right." He picked up a piece of chalk. "We can fabricate a custom joint a compensated scarf joint, reinforced. It'll be stronger than the original design." He looked at Noel, a challenge in his eyes. "If your blueprints are as good as you think they are, you can do the math. Now get me the new measurements. We're burning daylight."

The old man's stubborn, unsentimental competence was the jolt Noel needed. He raced back to his tablet, his mind alive with complex calculations. Fueled by a fresh surge of adrenaline, he redesigned the joint on the fly a brilliant, improvised solution born of pure desperation.

The race against the sunrise became literal. At 5 a.m., the sky outside the grimy mill windows began to lighten from deep, inky black to a bruised, pre-dawn indigo. They were running out of time. The last of the magnificent curved oak planks were hoisted into place, the final holly-leaf carvings glowing in the stark work lights.

With the final screw driven home, they all stepped back. In the center of the mill floor stood a miracle. The archway was magnificent a soaring, twenty-foot-tall structure of warm, curving oak laid over a powerful steel frame. The point where the two great curves intersected at the top formed a perfect, delicate pattern of holly leaves. It was a seamless fusion of strength and grace of bones and magic.

But there was no time to celebrate. The hardest part was yet to come. With painstaking precision, the crew maneuvered the massive archway onto a waiting flatbed truck. The first pale fingers of dawn were stretching over the mountains as the truck began its slow, nerve-wracking procession through the sleeping streets of Evergreen Hollow.

They arrived in the town square just as the sky turned a soft, pearly pink. The crane the same yellow crane that had symbolized Noel's initial, disastrous attempt was waiting. As his exhausted crew guided the archway and rigged it with cables, Noel stood there, a solitary, filthy, utterly spent figure in the center of the square.

The race was over. He had done it.

As the crane slowly, carefully lifted his creation into the air, the sun finally broke over the mountaintop. The first golden rays of a new day struck the top of the oak archway, setting it ablaze with a warm, hopeful light.

It was the most beautiful thing he had ever built.

He stood there, watching his grand gesture his impossible apology settle into its place at the heart of the town. He had built his bonfire. He had created a fire so bright he hoped it could burn away a decade of smoke and ash. But as he looked around the empty, silent square, a cold, hollow feeling washed over him. Holly was nowhere to be seen. He had built the bridge back to her. Now, all he could do was pray she would be willing to cross it.

Chapter 29

The Boy With The Sketchbook

Holly walked through a town that, for the first time, felt like a stranger to her. The joyful, festive energy she had worked so hard to create was now an alien landscape the cheerful music and laughter a language she no longer understood. She was a ghost at her own party, her heart a cold, silent void at the center of the celebration.

Her desperate search for Noel had been fruitless. His temporary office remained empty, his car was gone from his parents' driveway, and his phone went straight to a cold, impersonal voicemail. Every unanswered call every empty space where he should have been was another shovelful of earth on the grave of her hope. The evidence was undeniable. He was gone.

She had failed. She'd been a fool to trust him a fool to open her heart. But as Zara's words echoed in her mind *"Which story are you going to tell your grandkids?"* she knew her greatest failure wasn't trusting him; it was not trusting herself not being brave enough to fight. Now, it was too late.

She moved on autopilot, her feet carrying her toward the town square the epicenter of the Gala she was meant to lead. She needed to find Zara, to tell her she couldn't do it that she had to go home and hide from the wreckage of her own life.

She kept her head down, her gaze fixed on the snowy ground, trying to become invisible amid the happy, bustling crowd.

As she turned the final corner into the square, she heard it a sound not part of the festive music or the cheerful chatter. A collective, indrawn breath. A gasp of pure, unfiltered wonder rippled through the crowd, followed by a sudden, profound silence.

Confused, Holly looked up and her world stopped.

There, in the center of the square where nothing had stood the day before was a miracle. A magnificent twenty-foot-tall archway of warm, glowing oak, its perfect, soaring curve rising against the gray winter sky. Its design was as familiar as her own heartbeat: two massive, intersecting holly leaves the signature of their oldest, most sacred dream. The Evergreen Project.

It was impossible a ghost, a sketch from a dusty old box, a dream from another lifetime. And yet, it was real. Solid. A stunning, irrefutable fact standing in the heart of her town.

The crowd, which had been a wall of joyful strangers moments ago, parted for her as if sensing she was the one it was meant for. She stepped forward, slow and unsteady, her mind struggling to process what her eyes saw. The craftsmanship was exquisite the wood rich and alive, the curves flawless, the carved holly leaves so precise and full of love that her heart ached. It was the perfect fusion of a builder's strength and an artist's soul. The perfect fusion of Noel and her.

And then she saw him.

He stood at the base of the archway, a solitary, exhausted figure who looked as if he'd been through a war. His face was smudged with grease and pale with bone-deep weariness. His clothes were covered in sawdust, his hair a mess. But his eyes when they found hers across the silent square were filled with raw, desperate, unwavering love.

He wasn't on a plane to London. He was here had been here all night building this. For her.

The realization struck her like a physical blow, so powerful it buckled her knees. The packed bag. The half-written email. Her father's forgotten letter. It was the same story again a tragic opera of miscommunication, of two hearts trying to do the right thing and causing only pain. But this time, the gesture wasn't a lost letter. It was a twenty-foot monument to his love, his commitment, his choice. A fire so bright it burned away every last shadow of doubt.

She started walking again faster now until it became a run. The sounds of the town came rushing back, but they were different this time. They were the soundtrack to the most important moment of her life. She ran, her feet flying over the snow, hot, cleansing tears streaming down her face. She didn't stop until she'd crossed the last few feet that had separated them for a decade.

She launched herself into his arms, and he caught her his embrace desperate and life-affirming. She buried her face in the curve of his neck, breathing him in sawdust, coffee, and home and she sobbed. A great, shuddering release of a decade of pain, fear, and loneliness.

"I'm so sorry," she choked out, her words muffled against his coat. "I was so scared. I saw the bag, the email I thought… I thought…"

"Shhh," he murmured, his voice thick with emotion as he held her tighter, as if he'd never let her go. "I know. It's okay. I'm here. I'm not going anywhere. Not ever."

He pulled back just enough to frame her face with his hands, his thumbs gently wiping away her tears. "I quit, Holly," he said, his voice a calm, steady anchor in her storm. "I quit my job. I'm staying. There's no London. No other project. Only this. Only you."

"I love you," she whispered, the words a profound, absolute truth.

"I love you, too," he said, his voice cracking. "I love you more than I have words for. So, I built you this instead."

He leaned in and kissed her a kiss that held the weight of their entire story. It was a kiss of forgiveness, of reunion, of a future finally and irrevocably claimed. It tasted of sawdust, salt, and the sweet victory of a love that had, against all odds, endured.

Around them, a slow, tentative, then thunderous applause broke out. The entire town of Evergreen Hollow their silent, patient audience was celebrating with them. They weren't just cheering for the archway, the Gala, or the contest. They were celebrating two of their own, two halves of a story they had watched unfold, finally coming home.

As they broke apart, breathless and laughing through tears, Holly looked up at the magnificent archway the impossible, beautiful thing he had built for her. Then she looked at him the boy with the sketchbook who had become the man who could build dreams.

Zara had been wrong, she realized. It had never been about choosing between being safe and being brave. Because in that moment wrapped in his arms, her heart full of a love so deep and certain it felt like the foundation of the earth she finally understood. Loving him wasn't the terrifying choice. It was the only one that had ever made her feel truly safe.

Chapter 30

The Truth Under The Stars

The Evergreen Gala began not with a grand announcement, but with the soft, collective hum of a town coming alive. As the sun dipped below the mountains, casting the valley into a deep, velvety twilight, the lights of Evergreen Hollow flickered on one by one a constellation of their own making. The Old Town Bridge glowed with a warm, golden welcome, and the Memory Lane frames cast a reverent, gentle light along the path to the Town Hall. Strings of old-fashioned, oversized C9 bulbs wound through the town square, painting the falling snow in hues of amber, emerald, and ruby.

After the raw, overwhelming emotion of their reunion, Holly and Noel were swept up in the joyful whirlwind of final preparations. They moved through the last few hours before the Gala in a state of giddy, breathless excitement, their hands always finding each other amid the cheerful chaos. Their private reunion had become a public celebration their personal joy the spark that lit up the entire town.

By seven o'clock, the town square was a sea of happy, expectant faces. The air was thick with the rich, festive scent of roasted chestnuts from a street vendor, the sharp, clean aroma of pine from hundreds of garlands, and the sweet, comforting smell of hot cider and gingerbread served by Holly's tireless volunteers. The volunteer fire department band, in their slightly too-tight brass-buttoned uniforms, played a cheerful rendition of *"Winter Wonderland."*

At the heart of it all stood the magnificent archway a silent, powerful testament to a sleepless night and a decade of love. It was more than decoration; it was the town's new heart, a symbol of their shared dream made real.

Holly and Noel walked through the celebration hand in hand not as project managers anymore, but as part of the joy they had helped create. They were met with a constant stream of hugs, heartfelt thank-yous, and clasped hands of gratitude. Mrs. Gable, eyes glistening with tears, pressed a small hand-knitted ornament into Holly's palm. Silas Hemlock, in a rare display of festive spirit, clapped Noel on the shoulder and declared, "Good work, son. Good work."

They began a slow tour of their shared triumphs, seeing their plans through the eyes of the town they had fought for. They walked the Memory Lane path, now bustling with families. They watched as an elderly woman pointed to a glowing black-and-white photo of children building a snowman. "That one there," she told her wide-eyed granddaughter, "that's your Great-Uncle Charlie. He always had a crooked smile."

The past wasn't just being displayed; it was being woven, in real time, into the fabric of the present.

They stood before the Community Canvas now a masterpiece of collective joy. It was a riot of color and heart. In the center, a child had painted a charmingly crooked version of the bakery. Beside it, someone had written *"Evergreen Hollow Forever"* in elegant, looping script. They spotted Silas Hemlock's surprisingly detailed drawing of his old pickup truck and a series of tiny, colorful handprints from the kindergarten class. It wasn't the clean, professional mural Noel had once imagined it was a thousand times better. It was the town's soul made visible.

The warming hut was filled with laughter and steam families huddled inside, faces flushed with warmth and happiness. Through the window, they saw people sitting on Noel's heated benches by the skating rink, their faces glowing with delighted surprise. It was all working: the bones supported the magic, and the magic gave the bones a reason to exist.

As they watched the skaters, a woman with a sharp, intelligent face and a professionally curious expression approached them.

"Holly Sutton? Noel Bishop?" she asked.

"Yes," Holly said, her heart giving a nervous flutter.

"I'm Catherine Albright," the woman said, extending a hand. "From the *New England Chronicle* blog. I received your invitation."

"Ms. Albright," Noel said warmly, shaking her hand. "We're so glad you could make it. Welcome to Evergreen Hollow."

There was no defensiveness in their greeting, only a quiet, unshakable confidence. Ms. Albright seemed momentarily taken aback, her cynical journalist's armor slightly dented by their genuine warmth.

"It's… quite a celebration," she admitted, her eyes taking in the vibrant, joyful scene.

"Let us show you around," Holly said, her smile bright and sincere.

Just as they began to walk, a ripple of nervous excitement passed through the crowd. A small group of people two men and a woman in dark overcoats, clipboards in hand had arrived at the edge of the square. The judges. The final arbiters of their fate. They began their slow, methodical walk through the town, their faces professional and unreadable.

The final act of the evening the culmination of all their work was at hand.

Mayor Thompson took the stage, his face beaming, his voice thick with emotion as he welcomed everyone.

"Tonight," he began, his voice booming across the square, "we're celebrating more than just Christmas. We're celebrating this town its heart, its history, and the hope that makes this place so special. And we're celebrating the two people who reminded us what we're capable of when we work together." He gestured toward Holly and Noel. "And they have one last surprise for us all."

Holly and Noel stood side by side at the edge of the stage. Noel held his tablet, his thumb hovering over the final command. They looked at each other a universe of shared history, struggle, and triumph passing between them in a single, silent glance.

He nodded. She smiled.

He pressed the screen.

For a moment, there was only the dark, familiar stone façade of the Town Hall. Then, a single, tiny point of light appeared a seed of pure white radiance. It glowed, pulsed, and then, with slow, breathtaking grace, unfurled a single green shoot reaching for the sky.

The entire square fell silent, a collective hush of pure wonder. They watched, mesmerized, as the shoot grew into a sapling, its branches spreading, leaves budding and deepening into a rich, vibrant green. The animation was slow, organic each motion imbued with the poetic rhythm Holly had envisioned. The seasons changed. The green gave way to the fiery brilliance of autumn, and then, in a moment of pure, quiet magic, the leaves didn't fall. They simply dissolved into a silvery-gray light, from which the first, perfect snowflake formed. Then another, and another, until the entire tree was glittering, its branches heavy with soft, glowing snow.

Finally, the magnificent, snow-covered tree dissolved not into darkness, but into a thousand star-like points of light that swirled and danced across the building. Then, one by one, those stars began to gather, spiraling toward the center of the clocktower, merging into a single, brilliant, pulsing star that shone out over the silent, awe-struck town.

A beat of perfect stillness.

Then the square erupted.

The cheer rose like a wave pure, unrestrained joy and pride.

Holly and Noel, momentarily forgotten by the celebrating crowd, slipped away, their hands finding each other in the darkness. Drawn as if by an invisible thread, they returned to their archway their monument. They stood beneath its soaring curves, looking out at the town they had saved, the sound of celebration a distant, happy chorus.

The sky above was a deep, cloudless black, glittering with a million distant stars.

"You were the magic, Holly," Noel whispered, his voice filled with reverence that made her heart ache. "All along. I just built the bones. You were always the magic."

"And you," she said softly, turning to him, her face illuminated by the town's warm glow, "you gave me the courage to believe in my own magic again. You gave me a blueprint for a future I was too afraid to dream of."

He leaned in and kissed her.

This time, there were no interruptions no ghosts of the past, no fears of the future. It was a kiss of profound, quiet certainty. The kiss of two people who had weathered a decade of darkness and finally, together, found their way into the light.

It was a forever kiss.

They held each other for a long time under the stars, beneath the archway of their shared dream.

The truth, the one that had been waiting for them all along, was now as clear and brilliant as the winter sky.

The prize, the contest, the judgment of the outside world all of it faded into insignificance.

The real victory was here, in this moment, in this town, in their arms.

They had already won.

Chapter 31

The Judges From The City

The morning after the Evergreen Gala felt like the quiet, contented sigh that follows a long, happy laugh. The frantic, joyful energy of the night before had settled into a soft, peaceful hum. A fresh, delicate layer of snow had fallen in the pre-dawn hours, blanketing the town in a pristine sheet of white. It muffled every sound, turning the remnants of the celebration the empty cider cups, the confetti-dusted snow, the magnificent archway standing silent in the square into a beautiful, cherished memory already.

Holly and Noel sat in the quiet of *The Rolling Pin*, the bakery not yet open to the public. They were utterly, profoundly exhausted, their bodies aching from a week of frantic work and a night of high emotion, but their faces were serene. They drank their coffee in comfortable silence, their hands clasped together on the old oak table a simple, solid anchor in the new world they had created. The contest, the prize money, the very reason for the whirlwind, felt distant and secondary. They had raced against the sunrise, faced their ghosts, and found each other. They had already won the only prize that truly mattered.

"Whatever happens today," Holly said, her voice a soft murmur in the quiet room, "thank you, Noel. For coming home."

"Thank you for being here when I did," he replied, lifting her hand to his lips and pressing a gentle kiss to her knuckles.

Their quiet moment was interrupted by the arrival of Mayor Thompson, his face a mixture of elation and sheer, unadulterated panic. "They're here!" he announced in a stage whisper. "The judges. And that journalist. They're having breakfast at the diner. They want the official tour to begin in thirty minutes."

An hour later, Holly and Noel stood in the town square before the three contest judges and the journalist, Catherine Albright. The judges were a formidable trio: a stern-looking man with a background in urban planning, a woman with the sharp, discerning eye of a design critic, and a younger man who specialized in community engagement. Their expressions were polite, professional, and completely unreadable.

Mayor Thompson began the tour, his voice booming with proud, paternal energy. He welcomed them to Evergreen Hollow and then, in a move of profound wisdom, stepped aside. "But I'm not the right person to tell you our story," he said, his gaze landing on Holly and Noel. "These two are the real architects of all of this. They are the heart and the head of our little miracle."

All eyes turned to them. This was it the final presentation.

"Welcome to Evergreen Hollow," Holly began, her voice clear and confident, devoid of the tremor of fear that had plagued her only weeks ago. "We're so glad you're here. We wanted to show you not just what we've built, but why we built it."

They started at the Community Canvas. The vibrant, chaotic masterpiece glowed with life in the bright morning sun.

"An interesting choice," the design critic, Lena, commented, her gaze sweeping over the mix of childish handprints and heartfelt messages. "Weren't you worried it would look… amateurish?"

"We were counting on it," Holly replied with an easy smile. "We didn't want a professional mural that people would only look at. We wanted a conversation. This canvas is our town's signature. It's a little messy, it's a little chaotic, but it's all ours. Every person who lives here has a piece of themselves in this display."

They moved on to Main Street. Noel took the lead, explaining the technical side of their "Heartbeat of Main Street" concept. He spoke about the unified, energy-efficient lighting grid, the strategic placement of spotlights to highlight the town's Victorian architecture, and the clean, consistent bones of the design.

Then Holly provided the magic. She pointed out Zara's window a wonderland of knitted snowflakes and yarn-bombed candy canes. Zara, standing proudly in her doorway, gave the judges a cheerful wave. Holly pointed out the diner with its charming, retro-themed display, explaining that each window was a personal story, a unique expression of its owner, all united by the warm, steady glow of the lights.

Their next stop was the Memory Lane Project. The path to the Town Hall, lined with Arthur Vance's glowing oak frames, was even more beautiful in the daylight. The old black-and-white photos stood in poignant contrast to the fresh white snow.

"Each of these frames was handcrafted by a local woodworker, Arthur Vance," Noel explained, running his hand over the smooth, perfect joinery of one case. "He used reclaimed oak from the old town mill. He hadn't participated in a town event for twenty years, but he was a crucial part of this one."

Holly stepped forward, gesturing to a specific photo the one of Arthur's father in front of the clocktower. "We didn't want our history to be something you read on a plaque," she said, her voice full of quiet passion. "We wanted it to be a conversation between generations. This project has given our older residents a chance to share their stories, and our children a chance to see where they came from. It's not just about the past it's about connecting the past to our future."

As she spoke, Holly noticed that Catherine Albright, the journalist, was no longer taking cynical notes. She was simply listening, her expression thoughtful and intent.

Their final stop was the town square, where they explained the warming hut, the heated benches, and finally, the magnificent archway. Noel spoke of the structural engineering, the challenge of the overnight build, and the strength of the steel beneath the wood. Holly spoke of the dream it had come from, the symbol it had become, and the way it was designed to frame the Town Hall connecting their dream to the town's civic heart.

Their presentation was a seamless duet. He provided the *how*; she provided the *why*. They finished each other's sentences, deferred to each other's expertise, and moved as a single, confident unit. The judges' questions were sharp and probing about budgets, timelines, and community buy-in but Holly and Noel answered every one. Their combined knowledge was a formidable force.

As the formal tour concluded, Catherine Albright pulled them aside. Her professional, guarded expression had been replaced by one of genuine respect.

"I owe you both an apology," she said, her voice low and sincere. "My first article... I was lazy. I came here looking for a simple, cynical story about a corporate takeover, and I missed the real story entirely. I was wrong."

She looked from Holly's open, heartfelt face to Noel's quiet, steady one. "The story isn't about a town selling out," she said, her eyes bright with revelation. "It's about a homecoming. It's about a community remembering how to save itself. It's a love story for the town, and... well." She gave them a small, knowing smile. "My next article, the one that comes out on Christmas Eve, will tell the truth. I promise."

The resolution the professional and personal vindication was so complete it was almost overwhelming.

Finally, the head judge, the stern-looking man, stepped forward. He had been the most silent and unreadable of the trio. He looked around the square at the happy, hopeful faces of the townspeople gathered at a respectful distance, and then he looked at Holly and Noel.

"In my line of work," he said, his voice a deep, considered baritone, "we see a lot of towns try to win this contest. We see a lot of spectacular light displays. We see a lot of money spent. But it's a very, very rare thing to see a town's soul on display." He gave them a long, appraising look. "You've given us a great deal to think about." He shook their hands. "The results of the contest will be announced nationally on Christmas Eve. Good luck."

With that, the three judges got into a sleek black car and drove away, leaving the town in a state of suspended, hopeful silence.

The adrenaline of the tour faded, leaving Holly and Noel standing alone beneath their magnificent archway. The crowd had dispersed, their work was done, and the fate of the town now rested in the hands of the judges from the city.

"So," Holly said, a nervous, giddy energy bubbling up inside her. "That's it. It's over."

"It's over," he agreed.

She looked up at him, her heart so full she felt it might burst. "Do you think we won?" she asked in a whisper.

He looked away from the town, away from the project, and down at her his expression filled with a love so deep and certain it took her breath away. He reached out and gently cupped her cheek.

"Holly," he said, his voice a soft, steady truth. "We already did."

He was right. The hundred-thousand-dollar prize would be a miracle a lifeline. But the real miracle had already happened. It was here, in the quiet of the town square, in the proud, hopeful faces of their friends and neighbors, in the solid, unshakable feel of his hand in hers. They had won back their town's heart, and in the process, they had finally, completely, won back their own.

The race was over. Now, all that was left was to wait for the rest of the world to catch up.

Chapter 32

A Deed, A Key, And A Kiss

Christmas Eve dawned not with a flurry of activity but with a deep, collective, peaceful sigh. The Evergreen Gala had been a triumph a brilliant, heartfelt celebration that reminded every resident of who they were and what they were capable of. Now, a quiet, almost sacred anticipation had settled over the town. The work was done. The story had been told. All that was left was to wait.

In Holly's apartment, the morning was a bubble of quiet domesticity. The air was warm, carrying the scent of fresh gingerbread from the oven and the dark, rich aroma of coffee Noel had brewed. They sat at her small kitchen table, watching snow fall in thick, lazy flakes outside the window. This was their first Christmas Eve together in ten years, and the simple, profound peace of the moment was a gift more precious than anything that could be wrapped and placed beneath a tree.

Their conversation was light, full of the easy intimacy of a couple who had already weathered the worst of storms. They talked about their favorite childhood Christmas presents, about the terrible fruitcake her grandmother used to insist on making, about the simple joy of a quiet, snowy morning. The contest, the judges, the hundred-thousand-dollar prize it all felt a million miles away. Their personal victory the rebuilding of their love and trust was the only one that truly mattered.

"Whatever happens today," Noel said, his hand covering hers on the table, his thumb tracing gentle circles on her skin, "this right here has been the best Christmas of my life."

"It's not even Christmas yet," she laughed, her heart full.

"It is for me," he replied, his eyes soft with a deep, settled love.

As the morning wore on, the town began to stir. The announcement of the *America's Most Festive Town* winner was scheduled to be broadcast live on a national morning show at eleven o'clock. A large outdoor screen had been set up in the town square, right in front of their magnificent archway. Slowly, quietly, the townspeople began to gather.

Holly and Noel walked down to the square hand in hand and were absorbed into the gentle, hopeful crowd. They stood surrounded by the cast of their shared story: Zara, her eyes shining with nervous excitement; Mayor Thompson, sweating in the cold as he fiddled with the screen's audio; Noel's parents, their faces beaming with pride; even Arthur Vance, who had shown up in a clean flannel shirt, his usual grumpy expression softened by a flicker of hope. Frank Henderson stood at the back, his arms crossed, his expression unreadable but his presence was a quiet admission of his own investment in the outcome.

At precisely eleven o'clock, the faces of two impossibly cheerful morning-show hosts appeared on the screen. The crowd fell silent. The hosts launched into a dramatic, suspense-filled recap of the contest, showing clips of the five finalist towns. Then came a stunning, professionally shot montage of Pine Ridge's display a brilliant, glittering spectacle of lights and sound. A low murmur of anxiety rippled through the Evergreen Hollow crowd.

Then the female host smiled. "But the story that has captured the nation's heart," she said, "is the story of a small town in Vermont that rediscovered its own magic."

Catherine Albright's face appeared on the screen. Her new article had been published that morning, and it was a love letter. She wrote of Evergreen Hollow's *unshakable authenticity*, of a community that had *dug deep into its history to build a future.* They showed a soaring drone shot of the glowing Old Town Bridge, a close-up of a tearful woman finding her father's face in a *Memory Lane* frame, and a final, breathtaking image of the Town Hall projection the single, brilliant star of hope pulsing over the town.

"And now," the host continued, his voice booming, "the moment we've all been waiting for. The winner of this year's one-hundred-thousand-dollar grant and the title of *America's Most Festive Town* is..." He tore open the envelope. "Evergreen Hollow, Vermont!"

For a single, stunned second, there was absolute silence. Then the square erupted.

It was the sound of pure, unrestrained joy a massive, cathartic roar of relief and triumph. Strangers hugged, people cried, and hats flew into the air. Mayor Thompson openly sobbed into his wife's shoulder. Silas Hemlock vigorously shook Arthur Vance's hand. In the center of it all, Noel pulled Holly into his arms, lifting her off the ground and spinning her around. Their laughter mingled with the joyous noise of the town they had saved. When he set her down, he kissed her a deep, triumphant, public kiss that drew a fresh round of whoops and cheers.

Later that afternoon, after the boisterous celebration had settled into a happy hum and plans for the grant money were already being discussed, Holly and Noel took a quiet walk.

They followed the familiar path through the now-victorious town, ending up at their spot on the Old Town Bridge.

"We did it," Holly said softly, her voice filled with peaceful awe. She leaned her head on his shoulder, watching the river flow slowly beneath the ice. "We really did it."

"I told you we already had," he murmured, wrapping an arm around her. "This is just the bonus."

They stood together in comfortable silence for a long time, simply basking in the satisfaction of a seemingly impossible dream realized.

"I have a Christmas present for you," Noel said finally, his voice a low, nervous rumble.

"Noel, you didn't have to get me anything," she said. "You're the gift."

"Just this one thing," he replied. He reached into the inner pocket of his coat and pulled out a thick, folded, official-looking document tied with a red ribbon. He handed it to her.

Her brow furrowed as she untied the ribbon and unfolded the papers. It was a property deed. Her eyes scanned the legal language, struggling to process what she was reading. The deed was for the old, defunct Henderson's Hardware building the empty, ghostlike structure directly across the street from *The Rolling Pin.* And according to the document, the new owner was her. Holly Sutton.

She stared at him, speechless. "Noel… what is this? I don't understand."

He reached into his other pocket and pulled out a single, old-fashioned, heavy iron key. Pressing it into her palm, he said softly, "It's the key to your new office."

Before she could form a question, he drew one final item from his coat a rolled-up blueprint tied with a green ribbon. With a soft crackle of paper, he unrolled it.

It was a stunning architectural drawing of the old hardware store, completely reimagined. The ground floor was a bright, open-concept art gallery and community space. The second floor was a magnificent, light-filled design studio with two large desks, a drafting table, and a wall of windows overlooking *The Rolling Pin.* At the top of the blueprint, in a clean, elegant font, was the title:

EVERGREEN DESIGN COLLABORATIVE

Sutton & Bishop, Lead Partners

"I'm done with corporate architecture," he said, his eyes locked on hers, his voice steady and sure. "And I'm done living anywhere that isn't home. I'm officially moving my life and my new independent firm right here, to Evergreen Hollow. This will be our studio, Holly. Our space, where we can build whatever we want. The ground floor will be a gallery for you, for Arthur, for any local artist who needs a place to show their work. This is it. Our Evergreen Project for real."

It was his final, greatest gesture. Not a frantic, desperate race against the sunrise, but a quiet, permanent, deeply thoughtful plan for a lifetime. A promise of a shared future written in black and white, bound by a deed, and opened with a key.

Tears, hot and joyful, streamed down Holly's face as she looked from the blueprint to the man before her the man who had not only come home but was building a new one for both of them.

"Is this… is this real?" she whispered, her voice trembling.

"It's the realest thing I've ever done," he said.

The "kiss" of the title, she realized, was this the blueprint, the plan, the promise. It was the kiss that sealed their forever. And then, on the old, storied bridge, on a perfect Christmas Eve, surrounded by the quiet beauty of the town they had saved, he gave her the other kind.

He leaned in and kissed her a deep, passionate, unhurried kiss. It wasn't a kiss of rekindling, reunion, or forgiveness. It was a kiss of beginning a kiss that held the promise of a thousand quiet mornings, of a thousand shared blueprints, of a lifetime spent building a future together.

In the distance, the old church bells began to chime, their clear, hopeful notes ringing through the valley, calling the town to its Christmas Eve service. They held each other close, the deed and blueprint pressed between them their future finally, beautifully, and irrevocably designed.

Chapter 33

Christmas Eve

The joy that had erupted in the town square with the announcement of their victory was not fleeting or momentary. It was a deep, resonant, soul-affirming energy that carried through the rest of the day, transforming the town's hopeful anticipation into pure, unadulterated bliss. The hundred-thousand-dollar grant was a lifeline, a tangible tool for rebuilding but the title *America's Most Festive Town* was something more. It was validation. It was a declaration to the world, and more importantly, to themselves, that this small, quiet, stubborn town mattered.

As evening fell, a quiet, reverent mood settled over the valley. The townspeople, their faces still glowing with the day's triumph, made their way to the old community church for the traditional Christmas Eve service. The church, decorated with simple, fragrant pine boughs and the warm, flickering light of a hundred candles, was filled to capacity.

Holly and Noel sat in a pew near the front, their hands clasped tightly together Noel's parents on one side of them, Zara on the other. It was the first time Holly had attended the service since her grandmother's passing; the memory had always been too painful. But tonight, sitting beside Noel and surrounded by the warmth of the community they had fought for, it didn't feel like a place of loss. It felt like a homecoming.

The service was simple and beautiful. The choir, led by a beaming Mrs. Gable, sang carols with a joy that was palpable. The pastor spoke not of grand miracles, but of the small, quiet ones of community, of hope, and of love finding its way home. As the final notes of *Silent Night* faded into the rafters and the congregation stood to leave, Holly felt a profound peace settle over her a feeling of rightness so deep it felt like the setting of a foundation.

After the service, the community hall hosted a spontaneous celebration. The air was thick with the scent of Holly's hot chocolate and the happy chatter of a town reborn. It was here that the final threads of their long journey were tied up, one by one.

Mayor Thompson, his eyes still red-rimmed with happy tears, pulled them aside. "The council has already held an emergency meeting," he said, his voice thick with emotion. "The grant money is being allocated first thing next week. The garage is getting its new roof. Sarah Henderson's diner is safe. We're establishing a fund to help new local businesses open in the empty storefronts." He clapped them both on the shoulder. "You didn't just win us a contest you gave us our future back."

Later, as Noel refilled a thermos of hot chocolate, a figure approached him quietly. It was Frank Henderson. The man's usual cynical scowl was gone, replaced by an expression of deep, humbled sincerity.

"Bishop," he began, his voice a low grumble. "I... I was wrong. About everything. About you. About this contest." He looked around the joyful, crowded room. "I was so focused on the balance sheets, I forgot to look at the assets we already had our history, our people." He met Noel's eyes, and for the first time, Noel saw not an adversary, but a man who loved his town and was afraid of losing it. "Thank you," Frank said, the words clearly costing him a great deal. "For not giving up on us." He extended a hand, and Noel shook it firmly the gesture a final, definitive peace treaty.

A little while later, a cheer went up from a corner of the room where a small television was showing the late-night news. The headline was about their victory, but the secondary story was the one that caught everyone's attention. Catherine Albright's follow-up article had been an explosive piece of journalism. The news report detailed an official investigation by the contest committee into Pine Ridge's submission, citing "allegations of plagiarism and unsportsmanlike conduct." A quiet, satisfying sense of justice settled over the room. They had won not by slinging mud, but by rising above it.

In the midst of the celebration, Arthur Vance looking deeply uncomfortable to be at a party but undeniably proud found Holly. "That gallery you're planning," he rasped, avoiding her eyes. "I've been working on a series of hand-carved rocking chairs. From that cherry wood Bishop admired. I'd be... honored... if they could be the first pieces you display." It was the longest, kindest speech Holly had ever heard him give.

As the party began to wind down, Noel's parents enveloped them in a warm, four-person hug. Noel's mother, her eyes shining, cupped Holly's face in her hands. "Welcome home, dear," she said, her voice full of a decade of waiting. "We are so, so happy to finally have you both home."

It was nearly midnight when Holly and Noel finally slipped out of the back of the community hall and into the cold, silent, magical night. They walked hand in hand through the empty town square, their footsteps the only sound in the pristine snow. The lights of the gala were still on, casting a warm, triumphant glow over everything.

They stopped under their archway the monument to their story and looked up at the vast, star-filled sky.

"It's really over," Holly whispered, her head resting on his shoulder.

"It's really just beginning," he corrected her gently.

They stood in comfortable silence, basking in the profound peace of a journey completed. The whirlwind of the past month, with its ghosts and its battles, its heartbreaks and its triumphs, had finally settled.

"What are you thinking about?" she asked.

"I'm thinking about what color we should paint the walls in our office," he said, his voice full of quiet, happy certainty. "I was thinking a warm gray but you'll probably want something more cheerful."

"Definitely something more cheerful," she agreed, a happy, bubbling laugh escaping her.

They talked about the small, beautiful, ordinary details of the life waiting for them. It was a conversation so full of hope, so full of a future she had never allowed herself to imagine, that it made her heart ache with joy.

He turned to her, his expression serious, his eyes full of a love as deep and endless as the night sky above them. "I love you, Holly Sutton," he said.

"I love you, Noel Bishop," she replied.

He leaned in and kissed her a slow, deep, peaceful kiss. It held the quiet joy of Christmas Eve, the profound satisfaction of their shared victory, and the unshakable promise of all the quiet, happy Christmases yet to come.

As they stood there, wrapped in each other's arms, the old church bells began to chime. Their clear, resonant notes rang out through the valley, announcing the arrival of Christmas Day. It was a sound of peace on earth, of goodwill, of a love that had finally and forever found its way home.

Epilogue

One Year Later

Christmas Eve, one year later, found Evergreen Hollow thriving. The *America's Most Festive Town* banner hung proudly across Main Street a testament not just to victory, but to a renaissance. The grant money, managed with the town council's fierce and loving pragmatism, had worked its magic. The old, empty storefronts were now filled with new life: a bustling bookstore, an artisanal cheese shop, a children's toy store.

Young families, drawn by the town's newfound vibrancy and old-fashioned charm, had begun to move in, their children's laughter a bright, new sound on the snowy streets.

The Evergreen Design Collaborative was now the beating heart of Main Street. The old hardware store had been transformed into a space of light, glass, and warm reclaimed wood. The ground-floor gallery was hosting its first annual Christmas show, a celebration of local artists. In a place of honor stood a collection of Arthur Vance's magnificent cherrywood rocking chairs, all of which had sold within the first hour. On the back wall hung a small but stunning collection of oil paintings depicting the quiet, snowy landscapes of Evergreen Hollow. The artist's signature was simple: **Holly Sutton.**

Holly and Noel were closing up the gallery for the night, the last of the happy, wine-sipping patrons having just departed. They stood for a moment, looking out the large plate-glass window at *The Rolling Pin* across the street, its windows aglow, a line of customers stretching out the door for last-minute Christmas treats.

"It's been a good year," Holly said, a contented sigh in her voice as she leaned her head against his shoulder.

"It's been the best year of my life," he replied, wrapping his arm securely around her waist.

Their life was a beautiful, chaotic, and deeply happy blend of blueprints and buttercream. They spent their days designing a new wing for the library, a restoration of the old mill, a new home for a young family and their evenings in Holly's apartment, their shared sanctuary. They had built a life that was both bigger and smaller than they had ever dreamed, a life measured not in accolades or budgets, but in quiet, shared moments.

"I have a Christmas present for you," Noel said, his voice a low, nervous rumble that made her smile.

He turned to her, and in the soft, glowing light of the gallery, he got down on one knee. He pulled out not one, but two small velvet boxes.

"I know we've already built our future," he said, his eyes shining with love and a hint of happy tears. "But I was hoping you'd make it official."

He opened the first box. Inside was a simple, elegant engagement ring with a single, brilliant diamond that glittered like a captured star. He opened the second box. Inside was a simple, strong platinum band.

"Holly Sutton," he said, his voice thick with emotion. "My partner, my magic, my home, will you marry me?"

Tears of pure, unrestrained joy streamed down Holly's face as she nodded, unable to speak.

"Yes," she finally whispered. "Of course, yes."

He slid the beautiful ring onto her finger, a perfect fit. She, in turn, took the simple band and slid it onto his. A promise for a promise. A partner for a partner.

He stood and pulled her into his arms, kissing her just as the old church bells began to chime, their clear, hopeful notes ringing out through the valley, announcing the arrival of Christmas Eve.

They stood there on the threshold of the beautiful life they had built together, looking out at the town they had saved, the snow falling in a gentle, perfect blessing all around them.

The boy with the sketchbook and the girl who kept the flame were finally, and forever, home.

Acknowledgments

A book is never built by one person alone, and this one is no exception. My deepest thanks go to my incredible editor at MK Storyworks, whose keen eye and unwavering belief in this story helped shape it into what it is today.

To my agent, for seeing the spark in a simple idea about a small town and a second chance.

To my family and friends, who endured my late-night writing sessions, read countless drafts, and always provided the perfect blend of encouragement and coffee, you are the foundation on which everything is built.

And finally, to every small town that refuses to give up, that fights for its history, and that knows its greatest asset will always be its people, thank you for the inspiration.

Author's Note

While Evergreen Hollow, Vermont, is a product of my imagination, its spirit is very real. It is a loving composite of all the beautiful, resilient small towns I've had the privilege of visiting across New England. The kind of places where the bakery is the town's living room, where history is cherished, and where community is not just a word but an action.

I hope that in our increasingly fast-paced world, we never lose sight of the magic that can be found on a quiet Main Street especially when it's decorated for Christmas.

Next Book Coming Soon

The Summer of the Tides

By Poppy Garland

For generations, the old lighthouse on Seal Harbor, Maine, has been the Abbott family's legacy. But for Liam Abbott, it's a prison. He's spent his life as the dutiful keeper, watching the world from a distance, forever bound to the light.

Dr. Cora Wells has spent her life chasing the horizon. A brilliant marine biologist, she arrives in Seal Harbor for the summer to study a rare pod of whales, bringing with her a world of adventure and a past she's trying to outrun.

When Cora's research boat is damaged in a storm, she finds herself stranded with the quiet, handsome lighthouse keeper. In the long, sun-drenched days and star filled nights of a Maine summer, two people from different worlds will discover that sometimes, the greatest adventure is finding the one person who makes you want to stay.

About The Publisher

MK Storyworks is a truly global book publisher, dedicated to the timeless mission of connecting compelling authors with enthusiastic readers across the world.

We pride ourselves on curating a diverse and dynamic list that spans the full spectrum of literary interests. Whether you are looking for an immersive escape into a bestselling fiction novel, seeking wisdom and knowledge from groundbreaking non-fiction titles, perfecting a dish with our acclaimed cookbooks, or introducing the magic of reading to the next generation with our enchanting children's books, MK Storyworks delivers stories that inform, entertain, and inspire.

Our commitment to quality, creativity, and global reach ensures that every book we publish finds its place in the hands and hearts of readers, no matter where they are.

Connect with MK Storyworks

Stay up-to-date with our latest releases, author news, and behind-the-scenes glimpses by connecting with us online:

Website: www.mkstoryworks.com

Social Media:

- YouTube: @mkstoryworks
- Instagram: @mkstoryworks
- Facebook: @mkstoryworks
- X: @mkstoryworks
- Pinterest: @mkstoryworks
- TikTok: @mkstoryworks